His name is

PATRICK DAWLISH

He is a very large man, six feet three inches in height, with vast shoulders that his well-cut suit cannot conceal. But for the broken nose, a legacy of an early battle in the boxing ring, he would be as handsome as he is massive . . .

He is always jumping in with both feet where the police fear to tread. And no thief, blackmailer or murderer ever comes up against a tougher, more resourceful, deadlier enemy than

PATRICK DAWLISH

John Creasey
as Gordon Ashe

A Shadow of Death

CORGI BOOKS
TRANSWORLD PUBLISHERS LTD
A National General Company

A SHADOW OF DEATH
A CORGI BOOK 552 08450 6

Originally published in Great Britain by
JOHN LONG LIMITED.

PRINTING HISTORY

John Long edition published 1968
Corgi edition published 1970

This book is set in Baskerville 10 pt.

Corgi Books are published by Transworld Publishers Ltd.,
Bashley Road, London, N.W.10

Made and printed in Great Britain by
Richard Clay (The Chaucer Press), Ltd., Bungay, Suffolk

CONTENTS

1

THE SHADOW

'Will it kill?' Mortimer asked.

'Within a few minutes,' answered Cotton.

'How can you protect yourself?'

'If you're in direct line with it then you can't,' stated Cotton. 'The only protection is the insulated container.'

The two stood looking at the innocuous-seeming piece of material. It was dull brown in colour, and not unlike a piece of coke or lava rock, though very much heavier. It was about four inches across and roughly oval in shape, but higher at one end than the other and with an uneven surface. It stood on a small metal table protected by a sheet of lead, and was inside a box made of a thick insulating plastic material, a box which had been specially made to keep in the lethal rays.

'What are you going to do?' Mortimer asked.

'Tell Sanderson, I suppose.'

'He'll want proof.'

Very slowly, Cotton nodded.

The two men were both of medium height and build, but there the similarity ended. Mortimer had a dark, sallow skin, thick black hair, and sharp features; Cotton was sandy-coloured and nearly bald, with blurred features and an almost cretinous appearance, which belied his scientific skill. Both men wore protective clothing, but each had removed his headpiece, which now hung down his back like the hood of a duffle-coat.

The laboratory was a small one attached to the main research department of a regional nuclear reactor establishment, and both Mortimer and Cotton were assistant physicists. Each man was concerned with the development of waste products after the smelting processes; the smelting by the nuclear reactors being simple enough, but the problem of the residual effect on the waste as yet far from overcome. Each worked entirely alone, without assistance; all the furnaces were electric and all the switch-boxes and fuses were outside the laboratories, which could only be entered with special keys.

Now, after a long pause, Mortimer said: 'What proof can you give him?'

'Look,' said Cotton.

He pressed a control switch, and a thick protective partition slid into position, cutting the box into two equal compartments, each almost square. There was nothing unusual in this. Most of these boxes, or containers, were sectional and with the help of magnets, mechanical arms, and other devices, objects could be shifted from one section to another. In this way many experiments could be carried out within the container with no risk of harmful effect on the men in the laboratory.

Cotton pressed another switch.

An opening appeared in the lead lining of the table showing a dark void beneath. The two men waited for several minutes, neither of them outwardly restless. Gradually, the head of a mouse appeared, a pretty little grey creature with pink eyes and an expression of puzzled interest. One was always kept available there for immediate experiment; when this one was removed another would replace it. It climbed into the section next to that containing the ingot. Less than a minute later it reappeared, then climbed back from where it had come, out of sight. The lead floor was sealed and Cotton pressed another switch. Immediately, a similar opening appeared in the lead lining beneath the section enclosing the ingot.

Slowly the mouse reappeared, and began to investigate. Suddenly its whole body twitched; as suddenly, it fell over on to its side.

Before their coldly watching eyes it began to crumple up, then, unbelievably, to shrink. A moment later it was only a tiny pile of ashes.

In a strangely matter-of-fact voice, Cotton said:

'It would take a few minutes longer with a human being.'

8

'My God,' breathed Mortimer. 'It was only in the other section for a few seconds. It didn't even *touch* the ingot.'

'It doesn't need to touch it,' Cotton stated, still in that matter-of-fact voice which nevertheless held a note of tension. 'Passing within its shadow is quite enough.' He paused, and pressed the switch which closed the opening into the second section. 'I've made one hundred experiments—this was the hundred and first. The hundred and first,' he repeated, and then his voice broke. 'I sometimes wish I could experiment on myself and see how long it would take to kill me!'

Mortimer looked into the other's shallow, wide-set eyes. 'You've kept this to yourself too long,' he said. 'Why don't you go and see Sanderson now?'

'I think I will,' Cotton replied. 'I should have told him before, I suppose. Do you know if he's in?'

'He's always in during the afternoon,' Mortimer said.

'If only he weren't so difficult to talk to,' muttered Cotton.

*　　　*　　　*

Professor Gordon Sanderson, the Head of the Midlands Nuclear Research Department, was a square block of a man with a bullet-shaped head and a thick, blunt jaw. He wore dark horn-rimmed spectacles, the eye-pieces rectangular in shape as if he took some satisfaction in emphasising the outline of his features. The features themselves were regular and small, except for his mouth, which was straight and narrow, like a trap. No one liked him, but everyone in the world of nuclear science and applied radioactivity had great respect for his intelligence, his integrity, and his knowledge. His chief short-coming was his inability to get on well with his fellow men. His subordinates regarded him with awe, his equals mostly with dislike, and his few superiors with tolerance. An immaculately dressed man, he kept his office almost excessively tidy; something about the room, as well as his manner, made nearly everyone who entered nervous of moving even the smallest object out of its place.

He sat now, as always, with his back to a wide window

on the second floor of the Research building. This was a comparatively new station in the country between Birmingham and Leicester, and the grounds had only recently been laid out. Green lawns and yellow gravel drives stopped half a mile from the building; beyond was open farmland, undulating and pleasant, with copses here and there, and a few trees on the distant skyline.

Cotton talked, and Sanderson listened with every appearance of attentiveness. But even now that he had nearly finished the recital, Cotton still wasn't sure that his chief was taking it in. The pale blue eyes were almost unblinking behind the dark spectacles, the stubby eyebrows seemed drawn together in a half-frown—which might in fact be a scowl of disapproval. Cotton's voice began to trail off, and he eased his collar. He was acutely aware of his unattractive appearance, and this awareness increased his lack of self-confidence.

'... and I decided it was past time I told you,' he finished. 'So here I am.'

It was a long time before Sanderson moved. Then he squared his shoulders and edged a little closer to the desk.

'*What* was the date of your first experiment?' His voice was hard.

'May the third,' answered Cotton.

'And it is now June the twenty-second.'

'Yes, sir.'

'That is fifty days.'

'Yes.'

'You have experimented twice each day?'

'Yes, sir. Once each morning, once each afternoon.'

'Using precisely the same heat, method, and crude ore?'

'Yes.'

Sanderson gave an almost imperceptible nod.

'Then you can hardly be in error.'

'I am not in error, sir.'

'Have you mentioned this to anyone except Mortimer?'

'No.'

'And you didn't mention it to him until today.'

'No.'

'I see,' said Sanderson. After a pause, he asked: 'Why didn't you inform me before?'

10

'I wasn't absolutely sure before.'

'I suppose I am responsible for that delay,' said Sanderson, making a rare concession. 'An experiment is not proved until it has been carried out a hundred times. Do you agree with that rule, Cotton?'

'It's foolproof,' Cotton muttered. 'Absolutely foolproof.'

'But so would fifty experiments be if they yielded identical results,' remarked Sanderson. 'You are absolutely sure that no one, apart from Mortimer, has a hint of this phenomenon?'

'Perfectly sure, sir. The experiments were carried out on my own, with materials only I indented for; only you and I have keys to that section of the laboratory and to that particular furnace unit.'

Sanderson relaxed slightly.

'You have certainly carried the experiments out with maximum security. What about your wife?'

It was characteristic of him not to know, or to pretend not to know, that Cotton was a bachelor. He almost certainly knew all that Security knew, and everyone who worked here was screened with the utmost thoroughness before being appointed.

'I'm not married, sir.'

'Family?' asked Sanderson. 'Friends?'

'No, sir, no one. I live on the station. I go into Nuneaton occasionally to see a film—and I went once to Birmingham to the theatre, five weeks ago. But always by myself.'

Sanderson frowned. 'You are a dedicated man, Cotton.'

'I've got my job to do, sir. And in this case I was simply carrying out an experiment following an accidental discovery—that this waste reduced all living tissues to ashes, even if exposed to it only for a few seconds.'

'Yes. I am impressed. How much did you tell Mortimer?'

'The results only, sir.'

'Why tell him before telling me?'

Cotton drew in his breath.

'Well?' Sanderson demanded.

'I've never found it easy to talk to you, sir. I suppose it was a kind of rehearsal.'

11

'You *have* been known to report,' Sanderson retorted drily.

'By written report in the first instance—verbal only in reply to questions.'

'I see,' said Sanderson. 'I see.' He reached out for a telephone and began to dial, still talking as he did so. 'Mortimer must be told to treat this matter as top security.' He stopped dialling and Cotton could just hear the ringing sound; it seemed to go on for a long time. At last Sanderson replaced the receiver, and looked straight at Cotton.

'How far have you thought this discovery through, Cotton?'

'As far as I think it goes,' Cotton said. 'It could be the ultimate weapon.'

'No more?'

'I can't find anything at all on the credit side,' Cotton replied.

Sanderson nodded, as if in agreement; without a word he stretched out for the telephone, dialled again, and waited. For a reason which he could not quite understand, Cotton felt his tension increasing, and questions thrust themselves into his mind. Why *wasn't* Mortimer answering? He seldom left the laboratory for more than a few minutes at a time, and there was a bathroom and all facilities close at hand.

Surely . . .

Surely there couldn't have been an accident?

My God! thought Cotton, supposing—supposing . . .

Sanderson replaced the receiver and stood up. 'We will go and see him,' he said shortly.

It was a long way from this building to the laboratory —down two flights of stairs, along several passages, out into the grounds, then through the lead-lined protection walls and into the research unit. They passed several guards and officials, but no one questioned these two men.

Soon they turned a corner in a wide passage. Three doors led off this passage to the right—the first opening to Mortimer's laboratory, the second to a laboratory the two men shared between them, the third to Cotton's.

Mortimer's door was locked. Without waiting to ring, Cotton strode on to his own, unlocked it, then stood aside for Sanderson to enter.

He hardly knew what he expected. These were almost meaningless fears that assailed him—why should he think that Mortimer would take the slightest risk? And yet he half-anticipated seeing his colleague stretched out on the floor.

The room was empty.

Cotton glanced at the door leading to the shared laboratory, then stopped in his tracks. Just in front of him was the container in which he had left the ingot, locked up and impossible to open without a key, as far as he had known.

The ingot was gone.

Cotton felt almost numbed with shock. Sanderson, who must have been quick to see the significance of the empty container, seemed shocked to stillness, too.

2

DEPUTY ASSISTANT COMMISSIONER DAWLISH

The Deputy Assistant Commissioner of the Criminal Investigation Department of the (London) Metropolitan Police was a large man in every way. Tall—over six feet three—and very broad and massive, he had great breadth of vision and depth of judgment, and those who had known him all his life often remarked that the years had brought him even greater wisdom without any diminution of courage.

This was true.

Not that he, Patrick Dawlish, considered himself either wise or courageous, though he was quicker than he realised in calling other men fools. It was seldom, however, that he even thought of other men as cowards, for bravery, he knew, was a matter of a man's metabolism, and it often demanded as great a courage to refuse to be a hero as to be one.

In his early, army days he had been attached to Military Intelligence, which had demanded feats of great endurance, bravery, and acumen; it was said that he had parachuted behind enemy lines more often than any man alive—or, for that matter, dead—rescuing many from death, and sabotaging a quite remarkable amount of German war material.

Immediately after the war he had been restless and dissatisfied, and in the face of much opposition—including his wife's—he had become a champion of lost causes, a kind of private eye, undeterred by the disapproval of many policemen. A measure of his character and his calibre, however, had been proved by the fact that when the International Crime Conference had been brought into being he had been prevailed upon to represent Britain. That was when the rank of Deputy Assistant Commissioner had been created for him. Many had thought that he would chafe under the inevitable discipline, but he was adept at making himself master of any situation and this had been no exception.

The International Crime Conference was in constant session everywhere in the world, and was attended by delegates from each national police force. Sometimes it met in a European country, sometimes in the Americas, occasionally in India or in the Far East. Its purpose was very simple: the hunting down of criminals. In this age of speed, which rendered frontiers and oceans of little or no value in stopping criminals of one land from taking refuge in another, crime had become international: to defeat it, crime-hunters had to become international too.

Dawlish was a man dedicated to the fight against crime.

Very soon after he had met the other delegates at the first Conference he had realised that most if not all of them were equally dedicated. A newspaper reporter, attending a meeting, had been so impressed that he had dubbed them 'the Crime Haters', and the name had stuck.

Each delegate to the Conference, even when in his own

14

country, concentrated almost entirely on international crime. Every few months all the delegates met in sessions in one country or another—always under the chairmanship of the delegate in whose country the meetings took place. Here, knowledge was pooled—knowledge of the moves of criminals, of new methods of committing, preventing, and persecuting crime, of international crime rings, of the waves of crime which changed from year to year, sometimes from month to month. One year the greatest anxiety would be over drugs; another year, diamonds; another, forgery. Undoubtedly crime did come in waves, and far too often what had started as an isolated incident in one country spread quickly through that country, and on to its neighbours.

One evening late in June, Dawlish was alone in his office. It was a large one at the top of Scotland Yard, and magnificently equipped. On the wall opposite his desk was a huge relief map of the world, a Mercator projection which had been installed here by the British Overseas Airways Corporation, itself often involved unwittingly in many aspects of crime. The map's basic colours were green and brown, with varying shades for varying altitudes. The seven oceans were all pale blue, the higher mountains tipped with white. Built in behind the translucent plastic of which the map was made were hundreds of tiny electric bulbs. By pressing one of the forty-four buttons, Dawlish could light up any one of forty-four sections of the world.

None was alight now.

It was a beautiful evening and he was wondering what to do with it. His wife, Felicity, was visiting friends in Surrey, and he was to join her at the weekend. But it was now only Tuesday.

No particular crime wave was harassing the Crime Conference at this moment. There were hills or troughs even in crime, and it was not unusual to have a trough in the early summer. Summer, in fact, was often the slackest time in each of the hemispheres, for criminals had wives and families and enjoyed holidays as much as law-abiding men.

It was nearly five o'clock, Dawlish noted.

He could open another file and start tomorrow's work. He could go to his flat, collect his golf clubs and drive in the thick of the traffic as far as Richmond, and play golf.

Or he could simply go home and read.

And there were at least two attractive women to whom he owed dinner and whom he knew in London.

The last prospect pleased him, and he began to deliberate. Then, sharply across this delectable duty of decision, a telephone buzzed and a pale red light glowed on one of the three instruments within hand's reach.

All thoughts of dinner, feminine companionship, vanished; this call was from one of the Ministries, and from a top official if not a minister; and for any such to telephone him as late as this was rare.

He picked up the receiver.

'Dawlish speaking.'

'Oh, Mr. Dawlish.' The voice was pleasant, slightly laconic, very familiar: the voice of the Minister of Defence. 'I wonder if you could be at the Carilon Club in about twenty minutes' time.' He meant, of course, in exactly twenty minutes' time.

'Of course,' said Dawlish.

'I'm most grateful,' said the Minister, and rang off.

Dawlish replaced his receiver slowly and very thoughtfully. The Minister had uttered twenty-one words, might simply have made a social appointment, but had in fact told Dawlish a great deal. First, that he wanted the meeting to appear informal. Second, that it was of extreme importance. Third, that some kind of security was involved; and fourth, that he did not want even the most discreet of private secretaries to know anything about it.

The Carilon Club was in Pall Mall.

It was one of the oldest, largest, and most traditional of London's clubs, overlooking the royal Mall on one side, and approached by a private courtyard. Dawlish looked in at least once a week, so no one would be surprised at his presence there this evening.

The Minister was also a member.

Dawlish pressed a bell, and immediately Childs, his middle-aged, worldly-wise secretary, a pale, slightly jaded-looking man, came in from a door on the right.

'I'm taking the rest of the evening off,' Dawlish said drily. 'If there should be an emergency, try the Carilon

Club first and my flat afterwards.'

'I will, sir,' promised Childs.

Dawlish went down in the streamlined lift, walked through nearly empty passages to an empty foyer, out into the warm evening, crossed Whitehall and cut through Downing Street. Two or three tourists, their cameras poised, obviously hoped that he was some kind of political V.I.P. and were disappointed when he strode past the black door of Number 10. They were mollified to some degree when the four policemen on duty all acknowledged him. A woman's voice reached Dawlish's ears.

'I told you he was *somebody*.'

His back was towards her, so he could afford to smile.

He ran rapidly down the steps leading to St. James's Park, noticing with interest the crowds feeding the ducks on the lake; the old men sitting on the wooden benches; the lovers, heedless or oblivious of passers-by. So many people, reflected Dawlish, and each with his own private hopes and fears and worries.

He walked briskly, anxious to reach his destination without delay. What did the Minister want? he asked himself.

The Carlton Club seemed glad to see him. Two lesser members of the staff acknowledged him. Three of the club members nodded, but did not speak. A telephone rang, discordantly, and was answered with a haste which implied rebuke for so abrupt a disturbance of the club's sacrosanct quiet.

Dawlish went into the smoking-room; the Minister wasn't there. Selecting an *Evening News* from the rack, he sat back in an armchair from which he could glance up and see everyone who came in. A few moments later the Minister entered, tall, sharp-featured, and with a curiously sardonic manner. Dawlish allowed him five minutes, then followed him into the hallway which led down to the changing rooms. The club provided facilities for both swimming and squash-playing—it appeared that this evening the Minister was going to swim.

Dawlish stood at the edge of the bath, watching a man doing a racing crawl up and down as if training for the Olympics. A few moments later the Minister came out of a booth and saw Dawlish, as if by accident.

' 'Evening, Dawlish,' he said.

'Good evening, Mellor,' said Dawlish, swinging round with well-simulated surprise.

'Haven't seen you for some time,' remarked Mellor.

'Months,' agreed Dawlish.

The Minister nodded, poised on the side of the bath and dived in, making hardly a splash. Dawlish watched his long, lean body; the man must be sixty but he hadn't a spare ounce of flesh. *Did* he have his hair touched up? he wondered.

Collecting a pair of swimming trunks from the attendant, he slipped into the nearest booth, and five minutes later was flexing his muscles on the diving board. The man who had been doing the racing crawl came out of the bath as he went into it, and, as if alarmed by the illustrious company, scurried off to the showers.

The Minister trod water close to Dawlish.

'I think we have one of the deadliest problems ever known on our hands,' he stated simply.

'I hope you think wrong,' said Dawlish, as simply.

'I wish I could hope so. Do you know Gordon Sanderson?'

Dawlish recalled a dark-haired solid block of a man— a nuclear physicist. He began to feel alarm which the Minister obviously intended to create.

'Yes,' he said.

'Do you think he is an alarmist?'

'No.'

'He has alarmed me. Are you able to handle a mission personally?'

'Yes.' Dawlish gave the only possible reply.

'You've no commitments which would make you stop halfway?'

'I've one coming up in three weeks or so—but it could be cancelled if necessary.'

'Dawlish,' the Minister said, 'we haven't got three *days*. From this moment on, from four o'clock this afternoon in fact, we live, and have been living, in the shadow of death.' As if to give emphasis to his words, he turned away and swam with slow, deliberate strokes to the far

18

end of the bath. Dawlish slid deeper into the water, then floated on his back, and a few minutes later the Minister reappeared beside him.

'Sanderson will be at your apartment at seven o'clock,' he said grimly. 'Until then, he and other nuclear physicists are in conference with an assistant who discovered this . . .' He paused, then added with sibilant emphasis—'this *shadow*.'

Dawlish accepted the word 'shadow' without question.

'Can you give me any details?' he asked.

'I'd rather leave that to Sanderson, except for one thing. The shadow has been stolen.'

'Stolen!' echoed Dawlish. A laugh escaped him, he was so startled; and he had always had a strong sense of the ridiculous. 'Stolen?' This time he made it into a question.

'More precisely, the stone—perhaps a better word is ingot—which *casts* the shadow has been stolen,' the Minister said. 'Sanderson convinced me that you have only to pass close to this ingot to die within minutes. And he says that once the process is known, the ingot, which is constructed from iron ore with an infinitesimal percentage of uranium, is comparatively simple to make.'

'Who knows the process?' asked Dawlish, suddenly serious.

'The assistant who is with Sanderson now.'

'Will he be at my flat with Sanderson?'

'Yes.'

'Mellor,' Dawlish said. 'I hope you've made sure that nothing can happen to him.'

'The Special Branch are shadowing him,' the Minister stated. A moment later he too laughed, though without amusement. '*Shadowing*,' he repeated. 'Dawlish.'

'Yes?'

'It *is* deadly.'

'So I can see.'

'You must handle the search yourself,' Mellor insisted. Then, very quietly, he added: 'Don't fail us, Dawlish. Take any risk you must.'

Thank God Felicity isn't home, thought Dawlish.

THE MAN WHOM DAWLISH DISLIKED

Dawlish was back in his apartment high in a modern building overlooking the Thames, the neat span of Lambeth Bridge and the weathered red brick of Lambeth Palace beyond, the more distant arches of Westminster Bridge with its Victorian lamps and its throngs of people, cars, and huge red buses near by. The river looked smooth as a sheet of molten silver. The gothic towers and the castellations of the Houses of Parliament, newly cleaned, and palely brown, caught the evening sun in full light.

Up here there was no noise.

With Felicity away there was no staff on duty in the evenings, for Dawlish and his wife lived simply. Dawlish put out whisky, gin, soda water, and sundry other drinks, glasses, some cocktail biscuits from a tin which never became empty, and then glanced out of the wide window of this plain yet beautiful furnished room.

The buzzer, announcing that someone was downstairs to see him, broke gently on to the silence. Dawlish moved to a speaker built into the wall.

'A Professor Sanderson and another gentleman are here, sir,' a porter announced.

'Ask them to come straight up,' Dawlish said.

Aware of a positive but inexplicable feeling of relief, he went out to the lobby. This was the penthouse and there was only the one apartment served by this lift. The light over the doors showed that it was already on the move. *Eleven—twelve—thirteen—fourteen* flashed on and off, and then the doors slid open.

Dawlish recognised Gordon Sanderson at a glance.

He paid more attention to his companion, a man with fair lashes and eyebrows and indeterminate features. The pale, shallow-set eyes were steady enough, but the thick lips were parted in an expression almost of vacancy.

Dawlish stood aside, the two men stepped out, and the doors slid to.

'Good evening, Professor.'

'Good evening, Mr. Dawlish,' said Sanderson. 'I would like you to meet Dr. Cotton—Dr. Jonah Cotton.'

'How do you do, Doctor.' Dawlish held out his hand.

Cotton's grip was loose, his hand clammy. 'How do you do,' he murmured.

The words were slurred, and Dawlish's mind flew back to days when, engaged on a previous case, he had spent some time in a school for underdeveloped children, learning of their simplicity, their trustfulness, their tragic limitations. To look at, this man might be one of them, grown to adulthood.

Back inside his flat, Dawlish shepherded his two visitors to the sitting-room, closed the door, and moved across to the drinks. Every moment he was aware, almost uneasily, of the intense stare from those shallow eyes. Sanderson actually allowed himself time to go to the window and look out.

'A wonderful view,' he remarked.

'Yes, indeed. What can I get you?'

'Whisky and soda, please.'

'Dr. Cotton?'

'I—I don't so—thank you.'

'A soft drink—a bitter lemon?'

'That would be very pleasant, Mr.—Mr. Dawlish ...'

'Yes?'

'May I use your—er—your bathroom?'

'Of course.'

Dawlish led the way to a second bathroom off the main hall, leaving the sitting-room door open when he returned.

Sanderson reached for his drink.

'He's absolutely terrified, poor fellow.'

'I can see, that.'

'How much do you know?'

'The Minister isn't far short of being terrified, too. How about you?' Dawlish was pouring a second whisky, this time for himself. 'Cheers.'

'Cheers.' Sanderson lifted his glass, squinting down at it and pursing his lips after each sip as if trying to retain the flavour. For a few moments he said nothing, then, suddenly, he looked up.

'The stake is death, Mr. Dawlish. I've lived within sight of final dissolution for so long that I no longer get emotionally involved—but they have reason to be terrified. Do you want to hear the story from me first?'

'I'll wait for Cotton.' Dawlish poured out a bitter lemon, which fizzed with an almost vicious note. 'Unless you know the name of the thief and where he might be, and whether he knows the significance of what he has stolen.'

'Oh, he knows. His name is Mortimer—Eric Mortimer. He's an assistant physicist—the same rank as Cotton.' Sanderson was opening a black brief-case as he spoke, and he took out a file. 'There's his—dossier, isn't that what you people call it? I've no idea at all where he is, none at all.'

Dawlish opened the thick card folder.

'Were he and Cotton on this particular project together?' he asked.

'No. But Cotton made the fatal mistake of confiding in Mortimer when he had finished the experiments, but before reporting to me.'

'Most unlikely,' murmured Dawlish, uttering his thoughts aloud as he looked down at three photographs—one one print—of a dark-haired man with aquiline features, heavily marked brows, a bony, thrusting jaw; the bridge of his nose was almost pointed, it was so sharp. The whole face had the look of having been carved out of wood.

Sanderson started.

'I don't understand you,' he said sharply.

'H'mm? What is it you don't understand?'

'What is most unlikely?'

'I meant it is a most unlikely situation.' Dawlish looked at Sanderson straightly. 'Here is something of a deadly nature, the very shadow of which, so I am told, can kill in a few seconds. And Mortimer is supposed to have learned of it at the last minute. Yet, in a matter of moments, he is able to disappear completely, taking this ingot with him. He must have known about it already; must have been prepared in advance.'

'Yes. Yes, I suppose he must.' Sanderson spoke heavily.

'What about your security staff?' asked Dawlish.

'There was no reason for them to suspect Mortimer,'

Sanderson said.

If I had those so-called security men here I would fire the lot, Dawlish thought, but he made no comment.

At that moment the already open door was opened wider, and Cotton stepped through. Dawlish observed how quietly he moved, and realised that he might have been standing outside for several seconds—time enough to have heard the last few sentences at least.

'Ah, here we are,' Dawlish said, handing him the bitter lemon. Once again he was reminded of those under-developed children. 'Professor Sanderson has told me a little,' he went on, 'and I think I can take the deadliness of this discovery as read. A few quick questions, please. First, how can Mortimer carry this ingot about safely?'

'There—there is a small container—a portable unit.'

'What does it look like?'

'It's made to look like a typewriter case—it's very heavy, but then typewriters usually are.'

'What colour?' asked Dawlish.

'Black—the outside is a genuine moroccan leather.'

'Thank you. Are there many such in existence?'

Cotton glanced at Sanderson.

'The Professor knows more about that than I do.'

'We have several dozen,' Sanderson answered.

'All black?'

'No—they come in various shades of browns and reds and blues.'

'Is there any identifying mark on this particular case?'

'It has a code reference ZIK—beneath the handle and stamped on the metal feet.'

'Zik,' echoed Dawlish.

'It is Z-I-K,' explained Sanderson, 'and we call it "zik"!'

Dawlish got to his feet.

'Hang on a moment, will you?'

He went into a small room leading off the sitting-room, where there was a direct line to his office at the Yard, lifted the telephone receiver and dialled. The following moment he was speaking to Childs, who lived over the office.

'Dawlish here. Brief all police forces to be on the lookout

for a black moroccan leather typewriter case, with the code reference ZIK beneath the handle and stamped on each foot. It contains a radio-active metal. It could have been taken out of the country on any aircraft at any time after three-thirty this afternoon. Got all that?'

'Yes, sir.'

'At the same time alert all London and all British and European air terminals to be on the lookout for Dr. Eric Mortimer, five feet nine, medium build, sharp-featured . . .' Dawlish, still holding Mortimer's dossier, gave details of the physicist's address, home, and club, then went on: 'Send a messenger over for photographs, get copies made, send by teletype and then airmail to all police. Is that clear?'

'Yes, sir,' said Childs promptly. 'A red alert?'

'Yes.'

'I'll see to it right away, sir.' Childs knew that a 'red' alert to every police force in the Conference meant acute danger indeed, but he spoke as calmly as if he were discussing routine trivia.

Dawlish went back to the sitting-room.

'From now on, every police force will be on the lookout for the case and for Mortimer,' he told his callers. 'And now perhaps you'll give me more details of this discovery of yours.'

Sanderson nodded. 'Please proceed, Cotton.'

Cotton moistened his lips then explained in precise detail both the effects on the animals on which he had experimented and the possible effect on human beings. Once launched, his choice of word was good and his enunciation improved. Dawlish made no written notes but every detail etched itself on his mind. When the recital was over, Cotton began to perspire, dabbing his forehead with a grubby handkerchief.

'Had Mortimer shown any interest in your work?' asked Dawlish.

'Only—only to ask whether I'd had a good day or a bad one.'

'Did he have *any* idea of what you had discovered?'

'I don't know,' said Cotton helplessly. 'I just don't know. But he learned nothing from me until today.'

'Do you know if he had any money difficulties?' asked Dawlish.

Cotton's lips tightened. 'If he did he never mentioned them.'

'He had an expensive mistress—why don't you say so?' Sanderson demanded.

'I don't know anything about his private life,' Cotton insisted stubbornly. 'All I know is that if the shadow of that ingot touches him or anyone else it will kill.' Suddenly Cotton sprang to his feet and began to walk up and down the room, waving his arms, staring from one man to the other, 'What use is this talk, talk, talk. Why aren't we searching for him? Why ...?'

'That's enough,' Sanderson rebuked sharply.

'But if that ingot is taken out of its container ...'

'Dr. Cotton,' Dawlish interrupted, 'are you quite sure you didn't discuss your discovery with Mortimer before today?'

Cotton swung round on his heel.

'I've told you already—no, no, *no!*'

'Cotton ...' Sanderson began.

Dawlish interrupted him.

'I know what a strain you're under, Dr. Cotton,' he said soothingly, 'and I'm sorry I have to check and double check so much. Will you dictate a statement to my second-in-command in the morning, when you're rested?'

'*Rested?* How can I rest?' cried Cotton.

'As a matter of fact you'll have to,' Dawlish said. 'You need sedation and a sound night's sleep.'

'Sedation be damned! My God, are you *crazy?* I've got to be out looking for Mortimer. I've got to find Mortimer before that ingot does any harm.'

'Where would you look?' asked Dawlish.

'His house, his club, his friends ...' Cotton broke off, lifting his hands despairingly. 'Don't you understand, that ingot is deadly!'

'Yes, I understand only to well,' Dawlish said quietly. 'How *many* are there?'

'How many what?'

'Ingots.'

'But I've told you—*one!* Just one.'

'And you're the man who made it and knows how more can be made?'

'Yes, but . . .'

'Then we'll have to make absolutely certain that *you* can't get lost—or kidnapped,' Dawlish added, ignoring the other's protest. 'Mortimer and the one ingot might be a danger to anyone near him; you could be a danger to the world. Don't you realise that?' When Cotton simply looked at him, lips parted, eyes rounded, Dawlish went on: 'I'm afraid you'll have to be under protective surveillance for a few days, and leave us to find Mortimer. It's no use arguing,' he continued, as Cotton tried to speak. 'That's how it's going to be.'

Cotton drew in a deep breath, then said shrilly:

'You're a damn fool! You're crazy!'

4

THE THREAT OF THE SHADOW

The words fell on to the quiet room, so high-pitched that the last one was more screech than clearly uttered word. Dawlish stood stock still, wondering what was going on in this man's mind, what was driving and compelling him. Sanderson's brows drew together in anger, and for once he showed his feelings.

'Don't talk like that, Cotton. Apologise at once.'

'I won't apologise. He *is* crazy!'

'Cotton!' Sanderson moved forward, hands bunched as if he would use force, anger glowing in his eyes. But the younger scientist appeared oblivious of him, did not even glance his way.

Dawlish spoke mildly. 'What's crazy about it, Cotton?'

'You're like a child playing with fire! You don't know how to handle this. You wouldn't have a chance in a million—my God, don't you *see*? If Mortimer were in this room now and you were with him ...' Cotton's voice crackled, the stress of his fear was so great—'if you were in this room with him, you could be dead in a few minutes. He wouldn't have to touch you, just let the shadow fall on you. You'd be *dead*. That's how easy it would be!'

'We are well aware of the risk,' said Sanderson coldly.

'Then why the devil don't you behave as if you are?'

'Cotton, this schoolboy rudeness ...' Sanderson began.

'Oh *God*!' exclaimed Cotton. 'Why don't they *see*? Why don't ...?'

Dawlish turned to Sanderson. 'I'd like to have a talk with Dr. Cotton on his own,' he said quietly.

'Really, Dawlish. But I have every right to be present, you know.'

Dawlish looked back at the older man, giving no indication of the sudden flash of exasperation that he felt. He believed he knew what was really going on here; these men were victims of the Establishment, prisoners of bitter internal differences, if not of antagonisms.

Sanderson looked exactly what he was: a solid block of a man, stubborn, almost immovable, secure in his authority and in the restricted world in which he lived. Cotton wasn't secure at all; Cotton was frightened—and a large proportion of his fear was due to his boss.

The issue at this moment was how to deal with Sanderson. If Dawlish were heavy-handed, asserting his authority to override the Professor's, it would only worsen the situation.

'Yes, of course you've the right,' he said diplomatically. 'But I know that the Minister would appreciate your fullest co-operation.'

He expected 'the Minister' to work like a charm. It did not. Behind their stubby lashes Sanderson's eyes reflected his anger, and his jaw set stubbornly. Dawlish had to bite his tongue not to show his own feelings. It was becoming obvious that this particular conflict was simply a stage in another, long-term one, a conflict exacerbated by the situation in which they now found themselves.

'Mr. Dawlish,' Sanderson said icily, 'this is an issue which involves the proper running of my department and

27

I insist on my right to be present during this discussion. I am not yet satisfied that I have heard the complete story.'

Dawlish pursed his lips—then, suddenly, he smiled.

'Looks like an impasse,' he remarked mildly. 'Let's have another drink.'

Taking Sanderson's glass, he turned his back on the two protagonists, opened a narrow drawer in the cabinet from which the drinks were served, and took out a small phial which contained several tiny white tablets. As he did so, he felt a nostalgic lift of excitement, a mingling of guilt and satisfaction. In the days before he had been a policeman he had used such methods without serious hesitation, but the activities of a senior policeman were proscribed.

Deftly he dropped a tablet into Sanderson's glass; it dissolved quickly in the generous tot of whisky which he poured on top of it. Adding soda, he turned back to the others. Sanderson had moved over to the window. Cotton stood where Dawlish had left him, his hands clasped tightly together, the knuckles gleaming whitely through the skin.

Sanderson turned from the window, took his drink, and drank deeply.

'We're both overwrought,' he said jerkily. 'This is a great anxiety. I'm sure Cotton had no intention of being offensive.'

Cotton glowered.

'You can imagine the danger if this discovery were to get into the wrong hands,' Sanderson went on. 'Dawlish —we *must* find Mortimer.'

'Everything we can do is being done.'

'Oh, nonsense! You've hardly ...' Sanderson stopped suddenly and gave a huge yawn. 'My God, I feel tired. You—you haven't been to Mortimer's home, you haven't ...' He yawned again, breaking off and staring at his glass, first with hazy hostility, then with sudden alarm. 'Dawlish, what did you put in ... ?'

Dawlish took the glass out of his hand before it dropped, handed it to Cotton, who took it mechanically, then saved Sanderson from falling. In the same movement he lifted the man in both arms as if he were a child, carried him out of the room, dropped him on to the spare room bed, and left him; he would be unconscious for several hours.

Cotton turned to face him as he walked back into the sitting-room.

'You—you must be fantastically strong,' he said thickly.

'Never mind my strength,' said Dawlish. 'Now—what is it you won't say in front of Sanderson?' When Cotton didn't answer, Dawlish's voice took on a new firmness. 'Get this clear, Cotton. I have absolute authority in this affair. Absolute. I don't know what you've done to antagonise Sanderson and I don't care. What you tell me will be in full confidence—the Professor won't know unless it affects internal security. Now, what is it?'

'I . . .' Cotton gulped. 'I've remembered something. Sanderson would—would fire me if he knew.'

'As a Government employee . . .' Dawlish began.

'He'd find a way of getting rid of me, he's always hated . . .' Cotton broke off, moved forward and for a moment was almost likeable. 'Can you imagine what it's like for *me* to get a senior post? A man who looks as stupid as I do?'

Poor devil, thought Dawlish, for the first time. Aloud, he said: 'It's how you behave that matters. What have you remembered?'

'I—I lost a key.'

'*Lost* a key?' echoed Dawlish. 'What key?'

'The key to my private laboratory.'

'Where you carried out these experiments?'

'Yes, I . . .'

'Could Mortimer have found it?'

'Yes—yes, he could.'

'So he could have followed the experiments stage by stage?'

'I suppose so, yes.'

'When did you lose the key?'

'About a month ago. It was a duplicate. I was always leaving it in my bedroom, and it's a long trek from there to the lab, so I made a copy. I—I do some turning and fitting in my spare time. I make model cars and aircraft.'

'Did you make this spare key against the rules?'

'Yes! If Sanderson ever finds out . . .'

'I don't see any reason for him finding out,' said Dawlish reassuringly. 'Now—where did you keep this duplicate key?'

'In the hem of my lab coat. I made a hole, slipped the key inside, then sealed it with sticky tape. The funny thing was that once I had a spare, I seldom left the other behind. I only had to use the duplicate twice.'

'Did Mortimer know about the duplicate?'

'He—he could have. The coat was kept in the central lab, and he might have noticed me take it out of the hem.'

'And you lost it about a month ago,' said Dawlish musingly. 'Did you ask Mortimer if he'd seen it?'

'No. It—it would have meant telling him I'd made it.'

'And you couldn't confide in him?'

Cotton gave a strangled laugh.

'Confide in Mortimer? He's climber-in chief, back-slapper-in-chief, he'd cut your throat if it would take him into a higher grade. God knows why I told him about the ingot—if I hadn't been beside myself with worry about telling Sanderson I'd never have mentioned it.'

Dawlish stared at this strange man steadily.

'Is Mortimer clever at his work?' he asked.

'Brilliant!'

'So he would deserve high grading.'

'For his scientific ability, yes, he certainly would.'

'Not as a man?' asked Dawlish.

'I don't really know him well enough to say. But I don't like him. I never have. There's something inhuman about him.'

'But you think it possible that Mortimer's been study-ing the effects of what you're doing,' Dawlish went on.

'Yes. Yes, I do.'

'Would he know *how* you've developed this—shadow?'

Cotton shook his head.

'Only—only by guessing.'

'Couldn't he read your notes?'

'There aren't any.'

'No *notes*?' Dawlish exclaimed in astonishment.

'I keep all the data in my head,' Cotton told him.

Dawlish looked at the thick mouth, the tiny, shallow eyes, hardly able to believe that Cotton's blurred features, his expression of near idiocy, could mask so incredible a mind.

'What are the chances of Mortimer stumbling on the secret?' he asked at last.

'It would be a chance—a chance in a million.'

'But obviously if he stole the ingot, he must have known it had a potential.'

Cotton nodded, helplessly.

'Tell me where I've gone wrong here,' Dawlish said. 'There is one ingot. It possesses a shadow ...' He paused. 'Could you call it a ray?' he asked.

'Yes, you could call it that. It's—it's more true to say that if you pass within its shadow, you will die. It isn't actually a shadow, but I always imagine it as one—as a shadow of death.'

'Is the power lasting?' asked Dawlish.

'I don't know. On the fiftieth day it was as effective as on the first, though.'

'So it could be. Is it quite safe inside the container?'

'Providing the container remains closed.'

'If Mortimer showed it to someone—demonstrated its powers of killing—could he do so without killing himself?'

'If he was sheltered by the container.'

'In other words, as far as you know the ray, or the shadow, has to fall directly on the victim?'

'That's why I call it a shadow,' explained Cotton. 'If it were radio-activity, for instance, it would permeate the air, in all directions. This doesn't. You can shut it off, and narrow its range by controlling the opening of its container.'

He was speaking with much more assurance, and glancing about the room, he stepped towards a silver cigarette box with a hinged lid. Picking this up, he brought it to Dawlish.

'Imagine this is the container—imagine the ingot is inside. Now watch.' He opened the box to its widest. 'Any living creature in direct line with the ingot would die. Anyone below or above the level of the sides of the box would be safe. Got that?'

'I've got it exactly,' said Dawlish. 'What puzzles me now

is why you're so afraid of it.'

Cotton stared. 'You can't be serious!'

'It can kill anyone within a direct line, all right, but so long as you keep out of that line you're safe.'

'Yes,' said Cotton, 'but where is the limit of that line? Bricks won't stop it. Steel won't stop it. Cement and stone won't stop it. And the further it extends, the wider its range.' He strode to the window, holding the box open so that the whole of the interior faced the river, the bridges, the embankment, the thousands upon thousands of people who were in sight. 'Everyone of those people would be affected,' he stated flatly. 'Everyone in the House of Commons. Everyone in Lambeth Palace. *Everyone*. Don't tell me you don't see the way it can be used.'

'Yes, I do see.' Dawlish spoke very slowly, very soberly. 'In the hands of a man who was prepared to use it, this ingot of yours could kill tens of thousands of people.'

'Yes,' said Cotton, 'that's it. You understand all right. And *I* discovered it. *I* had to stumble on a horror like this. And if it isn't found I'll have to live in the terror of its possible misuse for the rest of my life. For God's sake find it, Dawlish! You must find it!'

For the sake of thousands who could die, wondered Dawlish, or to salve whatever Cotton had for a conscience? But the reflection did him no credit and served no purpose. He had two tasks now.

To catch a shadow of death.

And to make as sure as he could that no more ingots could be made.

5

LOOK THREE WAYS

Cotton replaced the cigarette box and resumed his agitated walking up and down the room, while Dawlish let a dozen thoughts flash through his many-faceted mind. What was the truth about this man? Was he all he claimed, or was his nervousness due to something else, some other secret knowledge or secret act?

As if telepathically aware that Dawlish was thinking of him, Cotton suddenly swung round.

'What do you want me to do?'

'I want you to stay under strong guard,' Dawlish answered. 'I want to make sure no one can run away with you.'

'That I can't run away, you mean.' Cotton spoke bitterly.

'It will work both ways,' admitted Dawlish.

'What are you afraid of—that I'll sell to the highest bidder?'

'You might,' Dawlish said, and then added deliberately: 'If you're human.'

Cotton drew in a sharp, hissing breath.

'You're a comparatively poor man,' went on Dawlish easily, 'and a big enough sum of money might tempt you or anyone like you. You could also be tortured into telling what you know. Well, I don't propose to let anyone get at you for either experiment. Will it help if you work at the laboratory, or would you rather be somewhere else?'

'I'll go mad if I've nothing to do.'

Dawlish nodded. 'Then I'll make arrangements for you to be taken down to Nuneaton in the morning. No one will restrict your freedom more than they have to. It will be better if you're back at the laboratory. Anyone interested in you will expect to find extra security precautions but won't realise how intensely we're working if you carry on normally—though you'll have to concentrate on other research, we don't want any more of these ingots made. Cotton ...'

'Yes?'

'If anyone gets in touch with you, let your guards know at once.'

'How will I know the guards?' demanded Cotton.

'I'll have three men here before you leave, I'll introduce you, and they'll identify anyone else who takes over from them,' Dawlish said. 'Do you know Mortimer's girl-friend?'

Cotton moistened his lips.

'I've met her.'

'What's her name?'

'Wanda—Wanda Hordle.'

'Is she the type to goad Mortimer into getting more and more money to spend on her?'

'He doesn't need any goading to get it,' Cotton answered. 'He gloats over money. He might need a bit of goading to spend it.'

Quietly, Dawlish said: 'You hate your friend Mortimer, don't you?'

'What makes you think I don't hate everybody?' flashed Cotton.

That's my chief worry, thought Dawlish, you probably do. But he said nothing, and went into the next room to telephone instructions to Childs.

Twenty minutes later, three men arrived; men who would protect Cotton with their lives; should it prove necessary; and who would see that Professor Sanderson was taken home so that he would come round in his own bed.

*   *   *

As soon as they had left, Dawlish went back to his office at the Yard. Already a formidable pile of reports was waiting, reports that Mortimer had been seen in several different places. The one which seemed most likely was that he had caught a KLM flight from London Airport to Amsterdam late that afternoon, but all were being fol-lowed up. Special Branch officers were now searching his rooms at the Research Establishment; others were questioning his parents, who lived in Ealing, and his only brother, who lived in Bloomsbury and worked in a bookshop near the flat he shared with two other young men.

Dawlish chose to go and talk to Wanda Hordle personally; but before he went he arranged for Special Branch men to watch both the girl and the place where she lived.

*　　*　　*

Wanda lived in a sixth-floor flat in a fairly modern block in St. John's Wood. There was a doorman, there were thick carpets, there was an air of opulence about the place.

The doorman glanced at Dawlish's card.

'Quite all right to go up, sir.'

'Is Miss Hordle in?'

'Came in her usual time, about half past six, and hasn't left as far as I know, sir. Turn right at the landing.'

Dawlish nodded.

As he went up in the metal-sided lift, he had his second whiff of nostalgia. His job kept him tied to his desk more than he liked; at this moment he was like a bloodhound let loose on a scent. He turned right, and found himself facing a door with the word SIX written on it. He thought of ZIK. There was a bell on the middle of the door, which rang sharply and clearly when he pressed it. Standing back from the door and slightly to one side, Dawlish listened intently. For a moment there was silence, and he was tempted to ring again; then he heard a movement inside the flat.

A young woman opened the door.

She had a flowered scarf wound turban-wise round her head, and a loose-fitting towelling dressing-gown.

'You're early,' she began, as she opened the door. Then she saw Dawlish, and broke off in surprise, almost in consternation.

Dawlish made a mental note that the doorman hadn't warned her, and gave his most pleasant smile.

'Good evening.'

'Good *gracious*!'

35

'I'm sorry if I've come at a bad time.'

She tightened the knot in her dressing-gown cord. 'You couldn't have come at a *worse* time, actually. But how can I help you?' She had a pleasant voice, and despite the obvious disadvantage of being caught without make-up, she still looked attractive. Her eyes were big and a pleasing blue, her nose just a little snub.

'I'd like to have a talk with you, if I may.'

'I'm terribly sorry, but I'm just not free this evening. Who . . . ?'

'Scotland Yard,' murmured Dawlish. He smiled again, and showed his card.

She glanced at it, then drew back a pace; but there was nothing surprising in this, thought Dawlish, the word 'police' could cause alarm even among the most law-abiding citizens. After a short pause, she stood to one side.

'Then you'd better come in.'

Dawlish passed her, and she closed the door, ushering him into a small sitting-room. 'Do sit down,' she went on. 'I'm sorry if I seemed rude, but I thought you were some-one else.'

'Eric Mortimer?' suggested Dawlish.

She looked at him in astonishment. 'How did you know?' Then her surprise turned to concern. 'He's all right, isn't he?' she asked anxiously. Nothing's happened to him? He is coming?'

'I hope very much that he's coming,' Dawlish told her.

'What do you mean?' she asked sharply.

'I want to see him.'

'Why on earth should you—should the police want to see Eric? And why come *here* to see him?'

Dawlish chose his words carefully. 'I think he may be able to give me some information which . . .'

He was interrupted by a ring at the doorbell.

Wanda jumped to her feet, glancing quickly towards the door, then back at Dawlish.

'He hasn't got himself into—into difficulties has he?' she asked anxiously.

'If he's outside then he can answer for himself,' said Dawlish, rising also. 'Do you think that's him?'

'Yes.'

'Will you do something for his benefit as well as mine?'

'What—what do you want me to do?'

'Let him in without telling him I'm here.'

'What good will that do?'

'He might let out an involuntary remark that could be invaluable.'

There was another ring at the door.

Wanda looked troubled. 'I don't like it at all,' she murmured, as she hurried from the room.

It was by no means certain that she would do what Dawlish had asked, and he meant to make sure that if she warned Mortimer and he ran for it, then he, Dawlish, would realise what she had done in time to catch him. So he stood just behind the sitting-room door, watching the graceful movements of the girl as she ran along the narrow passage.

Would this be Eric Mortimer? he wondered.

Surely Mortimer would expect the place to be watched, in which case he would be most likely to send a messenger. By now, Dawlish felt certain that the caller would not be Mortimer, but he did not relax. If there was any hint that it might be a messenger from the physicist, then whoever it was would need following.

Wanda opened the door.

She did not speak at first—then, suddenly, gave a start. 'What ... ?' she began.

Dawlish saw the top of a man's hat, a black bowler, and the top of his forehead. That was all. Before he could move or cry out, the girl gave a curious gasping sound, and crumpled up before his eyes. The bowler had moved, the girl was pushed into the room, the man slammed the door and disappeared.

In the split second of shocked silence Dawlish could hear his footsteps as he ran along the outside passage.

*　　　*　　　*

There was the girl, in a heap on the floor; she might be dead.

There was her assailant—probably by the lift already. And Dawlish stood undecided.

Running towards her, he snatched up the telephone from a small table just inside the front door with one hand, then leaned forward and stretched out for the girl with the other. He touched her arm.

'Can I help you?' asked the operator.

'Tell the doorman to lock all the doors,' Dawlish ordered. 'There's a murderer in the building.'

The woman gasped: 'I'll sound the alarm, sir, everyone will know there's trouble, then. Who . . . ?'

'Try to make quite sure any side doors are closed,' Dawlish added. 'And send a doctor to Miss Hordle's flat, urgently.'

He put down the receiver and lifted the girl clear of the door, then swung it open and strode outside, but the lift doors were closed and there was no one in sight. As he reached the lift he saw the indicator showing 'G'. So the man was already at the ground floor. He pressed the button for the lift and drew back. As he had come in he had made a mental, almost subconscious, note of the layout of the building. Wanda Hordle's apartment was at the back, so an apartment near the lift on the opposite side of the passage must overlook the front. He rang the bell. At last luck was with him, for it was opened at once by a plump, homely looking little woman, grey-haired, kindly faced.

She smiled. 'Good evening. What can I . . . ?'

'I'm from the police,' Dawlish said bluntly. 'I need to look out of a front window, quickly.' He stepped inside and the woman stared at him, eyes rounded with surprise. Voices, from television or radio, sounded from a room on his right. 'Please go and help Miss Hordle in the opposite apartment—she's badly hurt,' he went on, and pushed open a door.

A bald-headed man in shirt-sleeves was getting out of a chair, opposite a television set. The windows, which stretched almost all the way across the room, obviously faced the street, and one was ajar. Dawlish strode towards it, as the man exclaimed:

'Here, who . . . ?'

Dawlish reached the window and pushed it wider open, then leaned out.

38

He saw moving cars, and people, and a cyclist.

He saw a man stepping into a stationary car.

He saw a Special Branch man at the entrance to the carriage-way.

Putting his fingers to his lips, Dawlish emitted an ear-splitting whistle. Everyone in sight looked up, including the Special Branch man. Dawlish leaned dangerously out of the window, hoping to be recognised, stabbing his finger in the direction of the car which was beginning to move away from the kerb. The Special Branch man picked up his message quickly and sprang towards the car. The sound of his voice travelled faintly upwards but Dawlish could not hear what he said.

The man in the apartment reached Dawlish's side.

'What *is* this?' he demanded, as Dawlish drew back. 'What *is* going on? What ... ?'

The sharp sound of a shot cut across his words.

Dawlish, still looking out, was just able to see the Special Branch man—see him stagger, see him fall. The car into which the man had climbed made off with a sudden burst of speed. Passers-by stood and stared. Along the street were several other cars, anyone of which could have blocked the first one's path—but no driver made any attempt to do so.

The Special Branch man lay on the ground, half-on, half-off the kerb. Two men and a young girl ran towards him. Dawlish still looked down, his face set; the man by his side was now speechless. Only the television voices droned on and on—until there was a flurry of footsteps and the woman who had let him in appeared.

She was white-faced.

'Wanda Hordle's dead,' she said tautly. 'She was—she was stabbed to death.'

6

A GLIMPSE OF ERIC MORTIMER

Down in the street was a Special Branch detective, dead or gravely wounded; in the opposite apartment Wanda Hordle lay dead. These were the first victims of the shadow of death.

How many more will there be? Dawlish asked himself, a sick feeling in the pit of his stomach.

The woman came slowly, heavily, into the room, badly shocked, and the man sprang towards her, arms outstretched, glancing helplessly at Dawlish as he did so. Dawlish felt a keen sympathy for this harmless, humdrum couple, so suddenly caught up in the terrors of violence and murder. But what reassurance could he offer them?

'I've sent for a doctor, and detectives from Scotland Yard will soon be here,' he said gruffly. 'I'll be in Miss Hordle's flat.'

The man had his arm round his wife's shoulders.

'Come and sit down, Gwennie,' he was saying. 'Come and sit down.'

The woman was staring at Dawlish.

'But why?' she demanded. 'Why should anyone kill Wanda?'

The television voices had a marked American accent. Still they droned on.

Dawlish didn't attempt to answer, but went out, closing the door behind him. No one was in the passage, which seemed uncanny. He reached the open door of Wanda Hordle's flat and saw the girl lying on her back, where the woman had turned her from her side. The face, though slack, was still attractive.

Kneeling down, he felt for the girl's pulse, knowing it was useless. Yet it seemed wrong not to look for life.

As he did so, he heard footsteps, glanced up, and saw two men from the Yard and a young police surgeon; so Childs must have heard from the other Special Branch men. He beckoned and they came running, the doctor slightly ahead of the others, one of whom was a tall, big-boned chief inspector named Pole.

'There's a dead woman here,' he told them, getting to his feet, 'and another suffering from shock in the opposite apartment. Who's looking after things downstairs?'

Pole stepped forward.

'Lloyd, sir.'

'Who was shot?'

'Detective Sergeant Bennett,' Pole answered flatly.

'How is he?'

'He should live,' said the young doctor, bending over Wanda Hordle.

Faintly through the open windows came the sound of an ambulance bell. Everything would be looked after; the police machine was already in action, Dawlish simply had to feed it with the right materials.

He turned to Pole.

'The killer was a man about five feet nine, wearing dark clothes and a bowler. He got away in a black Austin Princess. The car turned left at the end of this road, into St. John's Wood Road, apparently heading for the West End. Bennett almost certainly had a clear view of him —so did this woman, whose name is Wanda Hordle.'

'A friend of Eric Mortimer,' said Pole, ruminatively.

'Yes. Is there any word of Mortimer?'

'There's a reliable report that he was seen boarding an Air France plane at London Airport,' answered Pole. 'It was a Paris flight.'

Dawlish grunted.

'I'm going to have a look round here,' he said. 'You put things in hand—but use a telephone in another apartment.' He lifted Wanda Hordle's receiver, as the doctor rose from the body.

'Death was instantaneous,' the doctor announced. 'The killer certainly knew his anatomy.'

'So I gathered.' Dawlish was dialling. 'Childs ... Get in touch with Pierre Cristal. Give him an idea what we're up against, and make sure he has Orly and Le Bourget airports closely watched, as well as any private fields around Paris. Lay on a plane for me, and tell him I'll be over before midnight.'

41

'I'll see to it, sir,' Childs promised.

'Is the evidence that Mortimer was on an Air France plane really conclusive?'

'There were three eye-witnesses,' said Childs. 'He was seen by one of our men and two airport policemen who thought he might be Cartwright, the forger—the descriptions are the same, but we know for certain that it wasn't Cartwright.'

'Was he questioned?'

'No, sir.'

'What name did he travel under?'

'Morton.'

'Where did he buy his ticket?'

'At the airport—twenty minutes before the flight took off.'

'Morton,' muttered Dawlish. 'So if it *was* Mortimer, then he already had a passport under an assumed name, and he must have been planning this for some time. What luggage did he take?'

'A brown canvas travelling bag, sir, and what looked as if it might have been a typewriter in a black moroccan case.'

'That's Mortimer all right!' exclaimed Dawlish. 'And to think we let him slip through our fingers! Well, it can't be helped, we'll just have to catch up with him. Don't let anyone take the slightest chance with Cotton,' he warned. 'If it ever looks necessary, lock him up in a prison cell. Have the newspapers been after you yet?'

'No.'

'They will be, after this,' said Dawlish, 'and they won't take long to associate Wanda Hordle's murder with her nuclear physicist boy-friend who's skipped the country. Tell them nothing about what's been going on—let them think our first alert was the attack on Miss Hordle.'

'Right, sir,' said Childs.

Dawlish rang off.

While he had been speaking, photographers and a full murder squad had arrived, and the little hallway, sitting-room, and a small bedroom leading off it, were now crowded with men and equipment. Dawlish went into a larger, very pleasant bedroom, with a few oddments of clothes draped about—stockings, an evening skirt, a black and white paisley scarf. In one corner was a writing desk, and Dawlish moved towards it.

On the top was a photograph of Eric Mortimer, on which was written, simply: *Love—Eric*, in a good, bold hand.

He had a forthright expression and an open countenance—the kind of man who might appeal to women, but one who did not fit the descriptions Dawlish had been given. He opened the drawers, found a bundle of love letters and put them aside; distasteful though the task might be, they would have to be read. There were a few bills, notes from friends, a bank book showing a credit of two hundred-odd pounds, some photographs of Wanda, and an address book.

There was a freshness, a cleanliness, about everything. And there was a poignancy in a letter, half-written, in a rather prim hand, presumably Wanda's:

Daddy dear, it was lovely of you to remember my birthday with such a *charming* present. I *love* my travelling clock, and now I'm away from home it's going to be especially necessary—but there's no need to tell you that!

What a relief to know you're well, and that Mrs. Smithers is looking after you properly. But, Daddy, it *is* time you overcame your prejudice against television. Eric and I have seen exactly the right set for you— one you can carry from room to room—and I *know* you'll become an addict once you start. There was a marvellous programme on stars and planets the other night, which you'd have loved.

So be prepared. I'd like to bring Eric down for the weekend (tell Mrs. S. *not* to worry about extra food) and we can bring the set with us. You don't need an aerial, don't need ...

Here the letter had broken off.

Dawlish was touched by the obvious *rapport* between father and daughter, surely a rare thing. Why had this girl been so viciously killed?

Why?

As he finished his search, finding nothing else of interest, and made his way out of the apartment and out of the building, another less urgent, and yet in some ways more disturbing, question built up in his mind. Who was going to tell Wanda's father? He would have to know soon, and he would also have to be questioned.

Flipping over the pages of the address book, Dawlish had discovered that he was a Major Gabriel Hordle, and that he lived in Devon, not far from Torquay.

It was a long way away, and time was limited—but perhaps if he, Dawlish, flew . . .

The idea, once in Dawlish's mind, began to grow. It was at least possible that Major Hordle would have some background knowledge of the true relationship of his daughter with Eric Mortimer.

Dawlish reached his office just after nine o'clock. It was still daylight.

Childs was putting a folder full of reports on the big, flat-topped desk; looking a little tired, perhaps dispirited.

'Have you eaten, sir?'

'No, I'll have a snack soon. Did you speak to Cristal?'

'Yes, sir—he's expecting you.'

'Any further word of Mortimer?' asked Dawlish.

'Report after report, but nothing new,' answered Childs. 'He wasn't seen in Paris.'

'Was he on the plane at Orly?'

'Yes, sir—checked off, and passed through customs,' said Childs. 'There's no word after that. Preliminary reports on his family have come in. Nothing remarkable. Mortimer is the odd man out—a brilliant son of mediocre parents whose other son is a fairly average citizen.'

'Debts?'

'He's a fairly heavy spender, but has a reasonable income which he supplements by writing articles and book reviews for scientific journals.'

'Gambling?' asked Dawlish.

'No trace.'

'Women?'

'No regular women friends except Wanda Hordle.'

'How long had he known her?'

'No one seems to know, sir,' answered Childs. 'She's quite a mystery.'

'Oh,' said Dawlish heavily. 'Is she?' He thought again of flying to Devon. 'What about her killer?'

'The car he got away in was stolen. The doorman saw him leaving, but only has a vague impression. Our man Bennett hasn't come round yet, but as soon as he does we should get a good description.'

'How is Bennett?' asked Dawlish.

'A bullet lodged in the ribs, close to the heart, but the worst thing is a skull fracture—he cracked his head on the kerb as he fell.'

'What about the owner of the car?'

'We had a bit of luck there, sir,' Childs answered. 'It belongs to a man who parks it regularly outside his office in a non-meter street not far from Marylebone High Street. He reported it stolen twenty minutes ago. He's being questioned now, but there doesn't seem any doubt that his car was selected by chance.'

Dawlish ran a finger down the bridge of his nose.

'I see. What about Cotton and Professor Sanderson?'

'They're back at the Research Establishment,' Childs told him, and when Dawlish made no comment for a few moments, he changed the subject. 'I've fixed the aircraft, sir, a three-seater. It's at London Airport, and we've a helicopter standing by to take you there. Cristal has booked you in at the Grand in Paris—he couldn't get you into one of your usual hotels.'

'If Cristal can't get a room, Paris must be chock-a-block,' Dawlish remarked.

'Will you have a meal here before ... ?'

'No,' Dawlish interrupted decisively. 'I'll have some sandwiches and a flask of coffee on the plane. And I'm going down to a Devonshire village named Bayton first. Call the Torquay police and ask them where I can land if Bayton is too far from the airport. And I expect I'll go straight to Paris from Torquay. I *might* get a bonus if I tell Wanda Hordle's father what's happened.'

Childs studied him thoughtfully, even solemnly, for several seconds.

'By breaking the news to the old man yourself you

might miss something in Paris, sir.' His voice when he spoke was curiously flat.

As flatly, Dawlish replied: 'All we've had of Mortimer so far is a glimpse. We're not absolutely sure he's in Paris —he could have gone in any direction from Orly. I want to talk to someone who knows him, outside his family— and Torquay isn't all that far by air from Paris. Don't forget to tell Cristal that I shall be late, will you?'

Childs smiled resignedly.

*   *   *

The flight to Torquay was smooth and pleasant, the pilot a young man who worked for one of the small charter airlines dealing mostly in commercial flying. The sandwiches supplied by the caterers at London Airport were far better than Dawlish had feared, and the coffee was hot. He finished a second cup as the lights of Torquay showed up, fringing the black void of the sea. Flares at the airport guided them in, and a black police Rover drew alongside almost as soon as the plane had stopped taxi-ing. Two men came from it, both in plain clothes.

'See you here in about two hours,' Dawlish said to the pilot, and climbed out of the aircraft almost into the arms of the two men.

'Mr. Dawlish?'

'Yes.'

'I'm Superintendent Soames, sir—and this is Chief Inspector Smith, who will drive you, if that's all right with you. He knows Bayton well. And he'll tell you what we've found out about Major Hordle as he drives. Is that all right?'

'Couldn't be better,' Dawlish said. 'On the whole, though, is what you know about Hordle good or bad?'

'Excellent,' the Superintendent said, 'but we can't say as much for his new housekeeper, a Mrs. Smithers. She's been inside at least twice for defrauding men she's worked for—a very *charming* person, we're told, but as crooked as they come. Chief Inspector Smith has the dossier on her, too.'

46

7

A MAN AND HIS HOUSEKEEPER

Dawlish sat next to Chief Inspector Smith in the Rover, the seat as far back as it would go, his legs fairly comfortable. Through the starlit night they drove at a steady pace along narrow, twisting lanes with high hedges. Behind them was another police car with four men who, Dawlish knew, were to keep watch at Gabriel Hordle's cottage. The local police must wonder why, but Childs had certainly raised what the Crime Haters knew as a red alert.

'This Mrs. Smithers came down from London,' Smith was saying, 'and just after she arrived, we had word from a friend at the Yard to keep an eye on her. They knew her as Mrs. Hyde, and we identified her from photographs the Yard sent us.'

'Useful thing, co-operation,' Dawlish murmured. 'When did she come?'

'Nearly a month ago, sir.'

When the Cotton experiment was about twenty days old, thought Dawlish; when Eric Mortimer *could* have had some idea of what was in the wind.

'Do you know her?' he asked.

'I had her pointed out to me when she was visiting Torquay last week. She *looks* a nice old soul. Not so old, either—sixty-ish.'

'Do you know how Hordle got in touch with her?'

'He put a personal column advertisement in the *Telegraph*. The local chap at Bayton knew about that—he's pretty sound, sir, knows everything that goes on in the village. And he's keeping an eye on Mrs. Smithers.'

'The all-seeing eye of the police,' Dawlish remarked.

Smith spoke almost sharply. 'I've always thought we could do with more crime *prevention*, sir.'

'Couldn't agree with you more,' said Dawlish mildly. Just then he glimpsed some lighted windows. 'Is that Bayton?'

'Yes, sir. Major Hordle's cottage is on the edge of the

47

village, overlooking the bay. It's a lovely spot by day.'

'So I can imagine. Is Hordle hale and hearty?'

'One of these four-mile-a-day walkers, sir.'

'Not a bathe from the beach every day winter and summer?'

'No—there aren't many of those left.' Smith began to slow down, then took a sharp turn. 'We're nearly there. Will you go in alone?'

'Yes.'

'If you should need help . . .' Smith hesitated, obviously apprehensive.

'Give me half an hour, and come if you haven't heard from me by then,' said Dawlish. 'Are there many owls about here?'

'*Owls?*' ejaculated Smith.

'The wise old birds.'

'Er—I've never heard any.' Smith drew up outside a white painted gate, which led to a path and a small oblong shape against the stars. 'Here we are, sir.'

'If I need help before the half-hour's up I'll hoot like an owl,' Dawlish said, keeping a straight face. 'I'm quite good at it.'

'Are you, sir?' said Smith blankly. He got out on one side as Dawlish opened his door. The other police car had stopped some way up the lane, and the men could be heard taking up their positions.

Dawlish could just see the pale ribbon of a path leading to a white-painted front door. As his eyes became more accustomed to the darkness, he began to make out the shapes of windows, and he became suddenly aware of the heady perfume of tobacco plants or nightscented stock; he was never sure which was which.

He made out a brass ring-shaped knocker, too; and gave two deliberate knocks. Almost at once he heard a chair being pushed back, then a man's voice.

'No, I'll go, Jane.'

So Hordle called Mrs. Smithers 'Jane,' thought Dawlish. Footsteps sounded, a chain rattled, then the door opened, and the figure of Major Gabriel Hordle appeared. Behind him, Dawlish glimpsed a wooden staircase, and heavy oak beams in the white-painted walls.

'Major Hordle?'

'Yes.'

'My name is Dawlish. I'm sorry to call so late, Major, but I wonder if you can spare me a few minutes?'

'I've no doubt I can, but perhaps you will tell me what it is about, Mr.—did you say Dawlish?'

'Yes. I'm extremely sorry, Major—I'm afraid it's about your daughter.'

As he uttered the words, Dawlish almost hated himself. Wanda's letter had told of the bond of affection between father and daughter so clearly that he knew what a dreadful blow he was going to deliver.

'*Wanda?*' exclaimed Hordle, after a startled pause.

'Yes.'

'Is she . . . ?' The old man broke off, and stood aside. 'Please come in,' he said. He waited while Dawlish entered, head bent low, then went on: 'If you'll go into the room straight ahead, Mr. Dawlish.' He closed the front door but did not put up the chain.

Dawlish crossed a narrow passage and entered a long, white-walled room, the raftered ceiling too low for his comfort. There were brasses and bronzes, chintz and good furniture, every piece old and attractive. A pale-coloured Persian carpet stretched over wide, uneven boards of well-polished oak.

Hordle followed him.

'What is this message from my daughter?' he asked.

He had a fine face, thin, sharp featured, and a lot of white hair. Dawlish judged him as being a man capable of making quick decisions, and one moreover, who would not suffer fools gladly.

'Have you heard from her lately?' asked Dawlish.

'Not since last week.'

'Or from Mortimer? Eric Mortimer?'

The old man frowned. 'I do not hear direct from Mr. Mortimer, but I do hear a great deal about him from my daughter. Who *are* you, sir?'

Dawlish hated himself for what he had to say.

'I'm a police officer, Major.'

'A *policeman?*'

'Yes. And . . .'

'My daughter would never become involved in anything to do with the police!'

'I am afraid I have bad news for you, Major Hordle,' Dawlish said gently. 'Very bad news indeed.'

Hordle's colour faded. Dawlish wished that he would sit down, but he stood there stiff and upright.

'Please explain,' he said stiffly.

'Your daughter was murderously attacked this evening,' Dawlish said quietly. 'I can at least vouch for the fact that she had little warning, no real knowledge of impending death, and that she felt no pain.'

The old man stared at him.

'And I can also tell you that she was happy and quite free from fear up to the last moment of her life,' Dawlish went on. 'I am very, very sorry, sir.'

At last Hordle spoke. 'You are—very kind,' he said hoarsely.

He looked helplessly about him, as if seeking some kind of refuge, some kind of help. For a few seconds there was complete silence; then Dawlish heard a faint creak at the door. He did not think that Hordle noticed it.

The old man's hands were clenching and unclenching by his sides, and he seemed to sway. Dawlish moved towards him, ready to catch him should he fall.

'Major Hordle,' he said. 'We think that you may be able to help us find your daughter's murderer.'

Hordle stared blankly.

'Who might well have been an acquaintance of Eric Mortimer,' Dawlish went on. 'Has your daughter ever talked about Mortimer's associates, or business?'

'She—never talks—about anyone,' said Hordle jerkily. 'All I know is—that she is in love with him. She . . .' He put one hand behind him, as if groping for support, and touched the arm of a chair, but did not otherwise move. 'She—Wanda—*dead*. . .'

'Major Hordle,' Dawlish said, 'I know how she died, and it is my duty to find her murderer. I have come because you might be able to help. She had known Mortimer for a long time. Surely she talked about him, about his friends and acquaintances, sometimes?'

'No,' answered Hordle. 'No, we—had a strict understanding. Her life was her life and my life was mine. We did not interfere in each other's affairs. We helped each other if we could but we did not interfere. I know this man Mortimer is a scientist. That and only that.'

'Do you know him?'

'I met him only once.' Hordle put a hand to his forehead. 'I understand that there was some impediment to their marriage. I assumed he was already married, but I was never sure.'

'Did you like what you knew of him?'

'He was very pleasant when we met. A little perhaps' —Hordle paused—'over-indulgent towards the old.'

'Do you mean patronising?'

Hordle's grip on the chair tightened.

'What is the point of all these questions?' he asked wearily.

'I would like to know how well you knew Eric Mortimer,' Dawlish answered. 'You have my assurance, sir,' he added gently, 'that it is very important that I should know, or I wouldn't press you in these circumstances.'

'I hardly knew him at all,' stated Hordle flatly.

'Did you know what kind of a scientist he was?'

'A—a research scientist of some kind, I know no more. I . . .' The old man slowly lowered himself into the chair behind him. 'I—I would like very much to see—to see my daughter. If you can arrange that I will be very grateful.'

'Of course,' Dawlish told him. 'I'll have a word with the local police. They'll make the arrangements for you.'

'Thank—thank you. Now I must—I must rest. If you would ask my housekeeper to come in . . .' Hordle's voice tailed into silence.

Dawlish moved very quickly, for he had been waiting for a chance to see who had caused that creak. Swinging the door sharply open, he saw a woman straightening up from a crouching position. Dawlish did not show any indication that he knew she had been there, but followed her along the passage and into a small room on the left, beyond which he could see a kitchen. She turned and stared helplessly into Dawlish's face. Her own was pale, round, not unattractive.

'Well, Mrs. Hyde,' said Dawlish.

She gasped. 'Oh my God, you know!'

'Yes, I know. Go and help Major Hordle. When you're through, come back here. The cottage is surrounded.'

'I—I didn't plan to cheat him! I swear . . .'

'Your record won't be used against you if you tell me the truth,' Dawlish said. 'See what Major Hordle needs first.'

The woman gave him a frightened, sidelong glance as she passed him. Soon she could be heard talking, and Dawlish heard the old man's voice in reply. He went back to the sitting-room and paused outside the door; Hordle was telling her about Wanda, and she was saying: 'Oh, how dreadful ... What a terrible thing ... Poor, *poor* girl ... Let me get you a brandy, Major ...'

There were movements in the long room.

Dawlish went to the front porch, where Smith was standing; it must be over twenty minutes since he had come here. He closed the door behind him.

'Everything all right, sir?'

'I'll be talking to the woman, soon. I don't think he should be alone with her all night, though. Can you arrange for a doctor and a nurse to come here?'

'Got just the right policewoman, sir—and I can get a Dr. Mellow here within half an hour.'

'See to it, will you?'

'Straight away, sir.'

Smith went off to use the car radio and Dawlish went back into the cottage, feeling a strange, unwelcome sense of disquiet and distress. Without quite knowing why, he felt that he had handled the interview badly—had not been as gentle as he could have been. Or *should* have been. Slowly he came to the realisation that he was being driven all the time by a sense of desperation—he must find Mortimer quickly, must find the ingot which could cast so dreadful a shadow. In a way the need for urgency was de-humanising him.

Was that an absurd thought?

His introspection was interrupted by Mrs. Smithers, alias Mrs. Hyde, leading the old man upstairs. For a few minutes there were footsteps overhead, then she came down to the room where Dawlish was waiting for her. She saw him, and half-closed her eyes, as if she too had suffered a shock that was almost impossible to bear.

'How is he?' Dawlish asked.

'He's in bed. He—I don't care what you say, he ought to have a doctor!' She uttered the words defiantly, and a little colour returned to her cheeks. Some would think her a handsome woman, with her full lips and high-bridged nose, her fine if frightened eyes and upright carriage.

'One will be here soon,' Dawlish said.

She looked surprised, and was immediately deflated.

'Well, so long as there will ...'

'I've told you there will. And I've told you that we wouldn't rake up your past record if you tell me the truth. If you lie ...' Dawlish broke off, wondering whether she was really as unnerved as she seemed. 'Now, answer my questions, please. Why did you take the post with Major Hordle?'

'He—he advertised, and—and ...'

'You saw another nice old man you could swindle and cheat,' said Dawlish.

'No, I didn't, it's not true! I—I *had* to take the job. I didn't want to come so far away from London, but—but *he* made me.'

'*Who* made you?' demanded Dawlish, his heart beginning to beat fast.

If he could make her talk now, it might save days; might save lives; might help to catch Mortimer before any great harm was done.

She stood with her hands held out towards him, partly in appeal, partly to fend him off as if she were afraid of a physical attack. And because it was so important to make her talk, Dawlish clenched his great right hand and raised it slowly, the uncurled the fingers, large enough to encircle her pale neck.

'If you don't tell me who made you take the job I'll squeeze the life out of you,' he said harshly. '*Who made you take it?*'

'Mr. Mortimer!' she gasped. 'I didn't want to bury myself in the country, but he made me!'

8

NEWS FROM PARIS

If this woman who seemed so terrified was telling the truth, then Eric Mortimer had compelled her to come and look after Wanda's father. Why? In the few minutes while Dawlish stared at her and flung questions at her, this question came into his mind time and time again.

'Eric Mortimer?' he demanded.

'Yes!'

Why? Why? *Why?* wondered Dawlish.

'How could he make you come down here?'

'He telephoned me. He said he knew that I had a record, and that—that I'd done another job, one he kept quiet about.'

'What job?'

'For an old man who died.'

'What man?'

'You wouldn't know him,' Mrs. Smithers gasped. 'I looked after a Mr. Nash, he was a scientist, and apparently Mr. Mortimer had known him. I'd—I'd made a bit out of the housekeeping and borrowed a few pounds, that was all, but if the police found out I'd have gone down for another stretch. Mr. Mortimer kept quiet.'

Why?

'What did he tell you to do down here?'

'Look—look after the Major. And I have!' she cried. 'He's the nicest old man I've ever looked after, I wouldn't swindle him if ...'

'What else did you have to do besides look after Major Hordle?'

'I—I had to find—to find out ...' Her lips quivered and her voice cracked, but she made herself go on. 'I had to find out if Miss Hordle wrote or said anything to her father.'

'About what?'

'Mr. Mortimer's work.'

'And did she?'

'No, she didn't, and I told Mr. Mortimer so.'

'How did you tell him?' demanded Dawlish. 'He didn't call here very often, did he?'

Mrs. Smithers frowned. 'Only once, I believe, and that was before I came. No, I've never met him here—and he told me that if I *did* meet him I was on no account to mention our arrangement, Wanda, or anything I might have have discovered, even if we were alone. One never knew if someone were watching, he said, and if they were, then he might have to tell them about—about Mr. Nash. No, if I met him, I was to behave exactly as if there were nothing between us.'

'Then how could you pass on any information you might have gained?' asked Dawlish.

'He telephoned me once a week when the Major was in bed.'

'What was he afraid Miss Hordle might say?'

Mrs. Smithers lifted her hands helplessly. 'I don't know. I swear I don't know.'

Why should Mortimer fear that Wanda would talk to her father? thought Dawlish. What had the girl known that she could have passed on? As for Mrs. Smithers, the Torquay police could work on her, he decided, so could the Yard; he had found out all he was likely to at such short notice. There were anomalies and improbabilities in her story, but the main point was, that Eric Mortimer had deliberately kept quiet about a crime he knew she had committed, and then used her as a spy.

What did that make Eric Mortimer?

Dawlish looked very straightly at Mrs. Smithers.

'If you've lied, you'll regret it,' he told her bluntly.

'I haven't lied,' she insisted. 'I swear I haven't. What—what are you going to do?'

'If you've told the truth about this, then no one is going to rake up whatever you did to Mr. Nash,' said Dawlish. 'Did Miss Hordle ever say she was frightened of anything?'

'No, *never*.'

'Did Mr. Mortimer ever say he was frightened for her?'

'No, he just told me to find out what she said to her father, that was ...' She broke off. 'I ought to go and see if the Major's all right,' she went on, in a different tone of voice. 'He took two of his pills, he ought to be but ...'

'What pills?' Dawlish asked sharply, and it flashed through his mind that he should have foreseen danger to Gabriel Hordle and should never have allowed this woman to go upstairs with the old man unless someone else was present.

'He has some sleeping pills, he only takes them now and again. I gave him some hot milk to drink when he'd taken them. But I ought to go up to him now. I know you won't believe me,' she went on dully, 'but I like him. I really do.'

'We'll go and see him,' Dawlish said.

Old Gabriel Hordle was sleeping, and there was an empty tumbler, milk-smeared, by the bedside. He looked very peaceful, as if the strain had eased out of him as sleep had come. There was a startling likeness between him and his daugther, which Dawlish hadn't noticed before; the one in sleep, the other in death. Dawlish felt the pulse in the pale, frail wrist; it was beating steadily.

He turned away.

'If you think I doped him, you're wrong,' Mrs Smithers said. She looked down on Hordle with a softening of expression which made her appear quite maternal, then moved towards the door of the bedroom. As Dawlish followed her down the stairs, bending to avoid banging his head on one of the beams, there was a knock at the front door. Mrs. Smithers went ahead and opened it to admit Chief Inspector Smith.

'All right, Mrs. Smithers,' said Dawlish. 'You'll be asked to make a statement and sign it; be sure it tallies with the one you made to me.' As she nodded and went into the kitchen, he turned to Smith.

'Any news?' he asked.

'Yes, sir—there's a message from Mr. Childs in your office. He says your quarry has been seen in Paris. The French police are after him.'

*   *   *

As he flew over the dark countryside towards the blackness of the English Channel, Dawlish talked to Childs over the radio-telephone. It was now about half past eleven, less than six hours since he had first heard of the missing ingot.

'Is it positive identification?' he asked.

'Doesn't seem any doubt, sir.'

'Who's gone after him?'

'Pierre Cristal and two of his special agents.'

'Not talking too much, are they?'

'I spoke to Mr. Cristal and he assures me that he will treat the inquiry as top secret, and if the Press get on to him he'll handle it without giving the truth away.'

'Childs?'

'Sir?'

'Does he *know* the truth?'

'Only what work Mortimer's engaged on, sir, nothing specific.'

'Keep it that way,' Dawlish said. 'I'll call back, from Paris, but you go off duty. There'll be a lot to do in the morning.'

He rang off and sat back, letting his thoughts wander, from his interview with Cotton and Sanderson to his interview with the housekeeper, and her statement.

Why did he feel so sure that somewhere in what she had said there was a basic fallacy? Or falsehood? He did not know why, only knew that until he had some rational reason for Mortimer's behaviour, he would have his doubts.

Yet as she had looked down at Gabriel Hordle's peaceful face, there had been that unmistakable look of maternal love on her own.

Soon, the lights of a city on the French coast loomed closer.

'Le Havre?' Dawlish hazarded.

'Cherbourg,' the pilot informed him.

'It's altered a lot since my day,' remarked Dawlish, remembering nights when he had parachuted from aeroplanes not one quarter as airworthy as this one, behind German fortifications.

Why didn't men stop fighting one another?

Why, even in peace, were some men prepared to fight

society, and others bent on brewing conflict between great powers or power groups? *Why, why, why, why?*

Then he wondered whether the French police had in fact seen Eric Mortimer.

*   *   *

Inspector Pierre Cristal had no doubt at all that he was on the trail of the wanted man, and he was delighted for two reasons.

In the first place, he knew that Dawlish would not have sent out a red alert unless it was a matter of vital importance; in the second, he was particularly anxious to help Dawlish, who was well liked by the police of Paris.

Moreover, any problem concerning a nuclear physicist was a grave one.

Had this Mortimer defected? Had he brought with him valuable radio-activity *data*? Was he in touch with agents of hostile powers? Or was he simply hoping to sell to the highest bidder? Cristal, an alert, dark-haired, sallow-skinned man with flashing eyes, speculated as he watched the doorway leading to the courtyard of the house into which Mortimer had gone.

The discovery had been sheer coincidence—luck!—allied to swift police action once this luck had been recognised. Not only did Mortimer's description tally with that of Cartwright, the English forger, but it also tallied with that of a Paris thief who was wanted for a jewel robbery which had set Paris by the ears the previous weekend, and there was a report that such a man had been seen in this district—in a turning off the Rue de Rennes, not far from the crowded students' quarter of St. Germain des Prés. This turning was in near darkness, only two lights, in wall brackets, near by, glimmering. But the main road was well lit and a few yellow squares showed lighted windows. Traffic went past the end of the turning at a wild speed, and every now and again a horn sounded. Two or three youths strolled by, laughing at some secret joke.

It was a lovely, starlit night, warm yet unoppressive, as only Paris could be in the summer.

Pierre Cristal knew that there was another way out of

this house, but both exits were being watched by his men. He was alone here only for a few minutes while an agent had gone to check with the other watchers.

Luck, thought Cristal—and chuckled to himself.

The moment the report on the suspect had come in, he had hurried to the spot, hoping to apprehend the jewel thief. But one of the men who had seen the suspect being driven into the courtyard had been sure he was an Englishman. He had had a clear, leisurely view of the man as he had got out of the car, and from what he had said Cristal felt sure that this was the missing scientist.

Cristal could have raided the house immediately, but it was a red alert, and he must take no chances. And so, convinced that the man wanted so urgently by Scotland Yard was here, he had asked the Sûreté Nationale for help— and it had arrived within ten minutes. Now, hearing a sound, Cristal moved quietly forward.

He had always had one characteristic which was a grave fault in a policeman—an over-confident daring. There was no sense of vainglory, no showing off, not even desire for kudos, in the man. He simply liked to take chances, and in the past it had, on occasions, saved him a great deal of time and put many criminals in prison. Now he reasoned that this might be a good time to go and find out how many others were with Mortimer. After all, the house *was* surrounded, no one could get away unseen, and once they knew this, the criminals would hesitate to use violence.

He heard his own man coming back and as the other drew near, he whispered :

'Wait here. I won't be long.'

'But M'sieu l'Insp ...'

'*Wait*.' Cristal moved forward on the word, making hardly any sound on the cobbles. Peering cautiously through a window alongside the door, he could see a low-powered light in the hallway, shining on a wide, winding staircase. He opened the door a fraction; it did not squeak. He opened it wider, and stepped inside.

The quiet seemed deadly.

He went slowly up the stone stairs, leaning with one hand against the smooth wall. Reaching the landing, he saw a line of light beneath a bedroom door.

He stopped outside the door, listening.

Hearing the murmur of voices—men's voices—he drew back, a hand at his pocket, touching his gun. The voices seemed to draw nearer. He heard a sharp sound at the door, and pressed back against the opposite wall.

The door opened and, blinded by the sudden light, he just made out the shadowy figure of a man.

If it were Mortimer, then he must stop him, here and now. But he was in direct line with the open door, and was still blinded by the sudden light.

The moving figure receded.

The door *closed*—as if someone had seen him and was afraid.

Yet it had been done so quietly; so quickly; almost as if the door had been opened and closed simply to make him realise that he had been noticed.

That was Pierre Cristal's last coherent thought.

As it passed, something seemed to sag inside him; he was suddenly in the grip of a terrible fatigue: legs, arms, body, all of him so overwhelmingly tired—exhausted— that it was like becoming a victim of a sudden, furious on-slaught of *la grippe*.

From that moment on, he knew nothing.

He did not even know that his body crumpled up, be-ginning to disintegrate as it touched the ground.

9

ASHES TO ASHES

Dawlish stepped out of the aircraft at Orly Airport, ex-pecting to see Pierre Cristal among the people who surged towards him. The roar of a superjet, taking off, the roar of one landing, the bright lights about the airfield and the building, were all familiar to him and he hardly noticed them. A short, grey-haired man whom he recognised as a top official of the Sûreté Nationale was first among four men approaching from a car standing near by; another group ringed the aircraft, and as Dawlish neared the grey-haired man he felt almost as if he were being arrested, rather than made welcome.

The other's face was grave, but he extended his hand readily.

'I am glad to see you, M. Dawlish.'

'Good to see you, M. Ruhamel.' They gripped hands. 'How are you?'

'Very seriously worried,' declared Ruhamel.

'Has Mortimer escaped you?' Dawlish asked, and looking at Ruhamel's face, needed no answer to be sure that this was so, and more. Suddenly he felt a dreadful sense of failure, of hopelessness.

The Frenchman turned towards a large, closed American Ford.

'We must talk in the car—there we cannot be overheard.'

Dawlish nodded to his pilot, who was with two other plain-clothes men, and got into the car. Ruhamel climbed in beside him, and pressed a button; a glass partition rose, whining, between them and the driver, and this command of privacy set Dawlish's nerves even more on edge.

He began to fear what he would learn.

'M. Dawlish,' Ruhamel said, 'do you know what harm this Mortimer can do?'

'I have some idea,' answered Dawlish.

'Why were we not informed?'

'You were informed that he was extremely dangerous.'

'We were not told *how* dangerous.'

'I don't know exactly what you were told,' said Dawlish, 'but I'm quite sure it was enough to warn you that you should be extremely careful. What's happened?'

Ruhamel watched him in the light of the airport lamps as they passed—now bright, now subdued.

'Pierre Cristal is dead,' he announced.

Dawlish's throat went dry.

'How was he killed?'

'Do you not know?'

'I can guess. I don't know.'

'He—his body disintegrated.' Ruhamel spoke as if find-ing words was almost too much for him. 'He entered the house alone, and was missing for twenty minutes, so one of his men went to investigate. All he found was a heap of ashes, but some metal objects, in these ashes, including a ring and a tie-pin, were Cristal's. M. Dawlish, did you know that Mortimer could do such a thing?'

Dawlish nodded. 'Yes, I knew,' he said heavily.

'We should have had more warning,' said Ruhamel sharply, 'it was wrong to expose any of our men to such risk without enabling them to wear protective clothing. I cannot understand why you did such a thing—you, usually a man of such understanding.'

Dawlish leaned back and closed his eyes.

'Where did it happen?' he asked flatly.

'In a house near St. Germain des Prés. We are going there now.'

'Is anyone else hurt?'

'If no one else suffered that is hardly due to you.'

'No,' Dawlish said. 'No. Is the house surrounded?'

'Of course. All the occupants of the other apartments have been evacuated.'

'Where are—where are the remains of Pierre Cristal?' Dawlish asked.

'They have not been touched. Physicists from our own research departments have been sent for. Tell me this—now, please.' Ruhamel's voice was still cold and aloof. 'Is there danger in—the remains?'

'I know of none.'

'They are not radio-active?'

'No. I would have been told if they were. It is the shadow . . .' Dawlish broke off.

'You talk of *shadows*, m'sieu?'

Dawlish felt a flash of exasperation, but suppressed it. He could understand what was going through the French-man's mind, but of far greater importance than one man's anger and another's resentment was the danger of the ingot.

'I only heard about it late this afternoon. The ingot's ray is called a shadow. It has no other name.'

'So, what did you do?' asked Ruhamel.

'Within fifteen minutes of being told, I put out a world-wide red alert,' Dawlish answered. 'Since that moment I've been positively haunted by what might happen. And by the need to catch Mortimer.' He pressed his hand against his forehead. The car went on without pause, and for the first time he realised that they were under a motor-cycle escort. He did not recognise the district, but they were nearing the heart of Paris.

'If we had been warned in time ...'

'Shall we concentrate on Mortimer and where he might be?' said Dawlish evenly. 'And discuss my shortcomings later?'

There was a tense silence, and for a few moments neither man spoke.

'We do not know where he has gone,' Ruhamel said at last. 'He was seen to enter this apartment. The house was surrounded and Cristal, who was watching the courtyard entrance, went in after him. When Cristal failed to return, one of his men went to investigate, and found him—dead. Mortimer had disappeared,' added Ruhamel, after a brief pause. 'He must somehow have slipped through our cordon. It is possible he was disguised,' he went on. 'Two men were seen in the street, but as neither looked like Mortimer, and our men presumed they had been allowed to leave by Cristal, they weren't stopped.'

You've done a hell of a fine job, thought Dawlish bitterly. He pictured Cristal, with his courage and his audacity: did it matter what happened to the body when life had gone? Yet Cristal had died because of his own great weakness, recklessness—and God knew who else would now die because of it.

But there was no more point in his feeling bitterly about Cristal than there was in Ruhamel blaming him, Dawlish.

'How much more can you tell me?' Ruhamel asked.

'It is simplest to regard it as a shadow,' said Dawlish slowly. 'The shadow of an ingot. This ingot is kept inside a special container, which is the only known defence against it. Once the lid of the container is opened, then whatever living creature is within direct line of the aperture is destroyed. Its radius is not yet known,' he added, 'but the ray, or shadow, of this ingot knows no barrier except the container. Once the lid is open then nothing can stop it; bricks, mortar, wood, stone, the shadow of the ingot can penetrate them all.'

'The shadow of the ingot!' breathed Ruhamel. '*Mon Dieu*! Is there to be *no* end to the evils these scientists produce?'

It was a question Dawlish had asked himself many times; and, as many times, had been unable to answer. To be followed by yet another question: did the good discoveries outweigh the bad, he wondered, or did the bad outweigh the good? But now, after the shock of Cristal's death, he felt in no mood for abstruse argument, even with himself, and with a non-committal shrug of the shoulder he leant forward and peered out of the car window.

They were driving past one of the bridges, and he could see the lights reflecting on the river, and the long, dark outline of the Louvre. A moment later they turned down a narrow one-way street, still under escort, left on to the tree-lined Boulevard St. Germain, then right, opposite the ancient church. Traffic stopped or pulled into the side to let the police car pass.

Soon they came to a barrier across the road, with two gendarmes swinging their white batons with great importance. The motor-cyclists stopped, the barrier was removed, a crowd already gathered on the other side of the road grew thicker. It was held back by a line of policemen.

As the car turned into a side street, Dawlish saw two big, black vans—vans in which the police of Paris drove at times of riots and parades. These vans were backed towards the Rue de Rennes, their head-lights full on. Several arc-lights were on, also, bathing the entrance to one of the houses in a pale white glare. More police stood outside the entrance, and inside the courtyard were two small cars.

The police car swung into the courtyard and pulled up; Dawlish got out one side, Ruhamel the other. A plain-clothes man whom Dawlish did not know saluted, and spoke to Ruhamel in French—too rapidly for Dawlish, who was out of practice, to understand.

As Dawlish joined them, Ruhamel turned to face him.

'There is a team of research workers at the apartment,' he translated.

Dawlish spoke heavily. 'M. Ruhamel, every policeman in Paris—every policeman in France—should be on the lookout for Mortimer. Every railway station, every airport, every seaport, should be covered as they've never been covered before. The research workers can make their own pace. We can't.'

Ruhamel pursed his lips.

'The same is true of Great Britain.'

'Mortimer was out of England before we knew what he could do.'

'I will speak to the Minister,' Ruhamel promised.

But when? thought Dawlish bleakly.

Was *he* doing all he could? he wondered. Shouldn't he talk to Childs—better still, to Mellor?

He followed Ruhamel into the house and up the stairs. Men were gathered at the first, small landing, three of them with a powerful light above their heads. They wore plastic protective clothing, including huge, lead-lined gloves—and they peered down at the heap on the floor.

Even Cristal's clothes had disintegrated.

His gun, some coins, the ring, and tie-pin which Ruhamel had mentioned, a penknife and some keys— these were there, but Dawlish could see little else. It was just possible to discern the crumpled shape of a man, and that was all. Dawlish saw how Ruhamel's face tightened, how his body seemed to grow tense; heard the hiss of breath between his lips.

One of the other men straightened up; he had a small box-like object in his hand, which looked like a miniature tape-recorder. He shook his head.

'There is no radio-activity,' he said, in the thick voice of a man from Alsace.

'Good. Then we may proceed with the pathological examination?'

'Yes.'

'We shall need an ambulance, something we can slide beneath the remains ...' The man talked on, coldly, dispassionately, and Dawlish noticed this but was much more acutely aware of the fact that somewhere in Paris, Mortimer was at large—with the ingot. While he was free and unchallenged there would be no danger to the police, but once he was traced and if he were surrounded, then, once again, he could use this ingot and cast its deadly shadow on anyone within its radius.

Dawlish shivered.

Stepping across the landing, he stood with his back to the doorway through which death had come so swiftly, so unexpectedly, to Pierre Cristal, and in his mind's eye he projected the direct fall of the shadow.

Ruhamel moved to a window.

'The courtyard,' he said, frowning. 'Do you think he went out that way?'

Dawlish went over to the window and looked out. Across the courtyard was another window, which was shuttered. It belonged to an apartment in an opposite building, also approached through the courtyard. He breathed hard.

'M. Dawlish, what is the matter, what is worrying you?' Ruhamel was suddenly agitated.

'Can we go and look in *that* apartment?'

'Is there any need?' Ruhamel asked, testily. 'Would Mortimer hide so close to this place?'

Dawlish didn't answer.

'You can't possibly mean that you think this shadow could ...' Ruhamel's voice trailed off into a muted: '*Tiens!*' Then more strongly he went on: 'We must find out. That must be Apartment 3.'

He, Dawlish, and one of the gendarmes, bounded down the stairs, reaching the courtyard as an ambulance backed into it. Crossing the yard, they entered the other lobby. An old man in blue dungarees, with a bottle of red wine, some bread, and some pâté in front of him, stood up from a table.

'Messieurs?'

'We would like to see who lives in Apartment 3,' said Ruhamel.

'That is Mme Boury and her two dogs, m'sieu.'

'Is she in?'

'She retires very early,' the concierge said, cautiously.

'Take us up to her, if you please,' ordered Ruhamel.

'She will be very angry if you wake her, m'sieu.'

'If she wakes, I will pacify her,' Ruhamel said sharply. He showed his card. 'Hurry, old man, and take your keys.'

The concierge moved surprisingly quickly for one so old, the metal tips of his boots knocking sharply on the stairway. Soon, they reached a door marked 3, and the old man rang the bell.

There was no response.

'The dogs do not bark,' the concierge said almost unbelievingly. He rang again, and still there was no response.

'Open the door,' Ruhamel ordered.

The concierge was now too perturbed to argue, and his rheumy, veined hands were unsteady as he turned the key in the lock. He pushed the door, but it was held by a chain. He drew back as Ruhamel took a knife from his pocket, opened a thin blade, and worked on the chain. Soon, it dropped heavily against the door.

Ruhamel nodded and the concierge moved forward. He groped for and found a light switch, which he pressed down with fumbling fingers.

Pale light glimmered on a hallway and three closed doors.

There was absolute silence.

Ruhamel went to the first door, Dawlish to the second. As he pushed it open, the hall light fell on the foot of a big, old, brass bedstead—and on a strange shape, which looked like a heap of ash, in the middle of the bed. Dawlish flicked on the bedroom light, and stepped inside.

The shadow had fallen on the woman and her dogs. Those parts of the bedding and bedclothes with which they had been in contact had also been reduced to ashes, but there was a fine-mesh wire mattress, which held the remains.

A prayer, oft-heard, passed through Dawlish's mind and he formed it now, with cold lips.

'Ashes to ashes ... dust to dust.'

This was the most dreadful case he had ever faced; utterly, unremittingly, horrifying.

10

THE RANGE OF THE SHADOW

From the moment he saw the ashes on the mattress, Ruhamel was silent. It was the gendarme who gave orders for the room to be locked, for the team now examining Cristal's remains to be sent here, for the concierge to return to his quarters and to say nothing to anyone. Throughout all this, Ruhamel stared first at the remains on the bed, then at Dawlish.

Suddenly it dawned on Dawlish that he himself must be behaving in the same way as Ruhamel: shocked into silence, almost numbed.

'That is everything,' the gendarme reported. Dawlish saw his narrow features, his tired eyes. 'Will you stay here?'

'I will go to my office,' Ruhamel said at last. 'You will come with me, M. Dawlish, please.'

'We have more to do first,' said Dawlish.

'I do not understand you.'

'We don't know the range of the—shadow.'

'Range?'

'It has already passed through three—no four, walls. This one, the outer one, and two of the other house. It has travelled forty of fifty metres. We need to make sure what has happened further along.'

The gendarme paled. '*Sacré Dieu!*'

'If we could get a plan of the district,' Dawlish began. His mind was beginning to work more quickly, and he went on: 'We don't have to do this ourselves, we simply have to find out ...'

'We have to find this Mortimer,' Ruhamel said sharply.

'And his accomplices,' Dawlish pointed out. 'M. Ruhamel, we need not only the police but also the army. Until now there has been an alert for a wanted criminal. Now we have a state of emergency.'

Ruhamel lifted his hands despairingly. 'It is a matter for the Government,' he said flatly. 'I will arrange for us

to be received. M. Dawlish'—he drew a deep breath—
'have you *any* idea where Mortimer might be?'

Dawlish shrugged helplessly. 'None at all.'

'Then he might be anywhere in Paris!'

'Almost anywhere in Europe, Dawlish thought bleakly;
and unless he were caught, almost anywhere in the world
within forty-eight hours. The same fear was obviously
in the Frenchman's mind, but he too was adjusting himself to the situation, and began to give orders.

Nearly an hour afterwards, Dawlish was sitting with
him in the office of the Deputy President of France, a
tall man with aquiline features and dark, brooding eyes—
a man who already carried heavy burdens.

'Yes,' he said, 'we have already been advised by your
Minister, M. Dawlish. It is obvious that there are two
matters of urgent importance. To find out how far the
damage has spread, and to catch this Mortimer. Everything—*everything*—is at your disposal. As you know
more of this—this *shadow* than anyone else in France, you
will be in charge.'

Ruhamel looked disapproving, but to Dawlish's surprise, he said:

'There is none better, provided he can command what
help is needed.'

'That will be arranged with the armed forces and all
branches of the police,' the Deputy President declared.
'There is an obvious password. *Shadow*. Use it and you
will get all the help you could desire, M. Dawlish. What
do you need first?'

'An idea of where Mortimer may be hiding,' Dawlish
said. 'There must have been some reason for his coming
to Paris. There could be other experiments at your own
nuclear research establishments.' He leaned forward in
his chair. 'First, this has to be an enormous police opera-
tion—but no one must know what it is about. The whole
populace would be terrified.'

'With that, I agree,' the Deputy President told him.
'Secrecy will be assured. It will be necessary to give the
newspapers some explanation, however.' He pursed his
thin lips, and Dawlish waited, beginning to seethe with
impatience but knowing the importance of deferring to

this man. 'We shall let it be known that Nato defence secrets have been stolen,' he said at last. 'That will be sufficient.'

'Will you confirm this with Mr. Mellor, sir?'

'Naturally.'

'Thank you,' Dawlish said. 'And now, if I can have an office, telephones, English-speaking officers preferably attached to the Conference, an open line to London and a staff which can sift all the reports that come in ...' He broke off.

'It will be arranged,' said the Deputy President. 'M. Ruhamel, you will be in charge of these facilities. Now, gentlemen, if you will excuse me ...'

*   *   *

There isn't time, thought Dawlish.

He felt a great and increasing sense of urgency, side by side with a sense of acute frustration. If only he could have directed operations from his own office there would have been so much more he could do himself. As it was, sitting in a large, barely furnished room in the building given over to the French delegates to the Conference, he felt that he was only marking time.

It was after three o'clock.

The sensible thing was to sleep, if only for an hour or two. He would need all his energy once results began to come in.

Sleep! The very thought was absurd.

Sleep! With Eric Mortimer and the ingot perhaps within a mile of him?

If there was only something he could *do*. Talk to Mrs. Smithers, for instance, she might know more than she had said—even more than she realised. And what a slip up for him, Dawlish, to have allowed Wanda Hordle to be murdered in front of his eyes. She had been so sure the caller was her lover that she had been taken completely by surprise. Had she known anything? Had Mrs. Smithers told the truth about Mortimer making her work for Hordle? If so, then Mortimer must have talked too freely to Wanda, and been afraid that she might pass on what

70

she knew to her father.

Would *he* have talked to anyone?

All such inquiries were being made, of course; Childs would see to it. There was nothing he, Dawlish, could do until a break came. God! What a case. He disliked Professor Sanderson, disliked the unattractive Cotton—though Lord knew he wasn't to blame for his appearance, poor devil. The only person in this affair he had liked at all was Wanda Hordle—and he had rather liked the photograph of Eric Mortimer.

Lucky fellow, to have such an attractive girl.

Why hadn't they married?

Old Hordle had talked about there being some impediment and had taken the situation quite calmly—more calmly than most people of his generation. What was the impediment? On Mortimer's side, or Wanda's? The only impediment to marriage, surely, would be if Mortimer was already married, as Hordle had suspected. There were other possibilities—loss of benefit under wills, for instance—but a previous marriage seemed the most likely reason.

He lifted the telephone with the direct line to London, and in twenty seconds he was talking to a young man named Carruthers, Child's deputy.

'... Yes, sir, we are checking. There isn't anything to suggest that Mortimer has ever been married, but there's a gap in the history of Wanda Hordle ... Not much we can do by night though, sir ... Yes, every friend, relative, and acquaintance of both Mortimer and the girl is being checked—and the same goes for Sanderson and Cotton ... We're fairly complete on Mortimer as far as we know.'

'Don't let's have any vagueness,' said Dawlish. 'Have you any record that he came to Paris recently?'

'He often took a weekend off and flew to Paris,' Carruthers answered.

'With Miss Hordle?'

'Three times with and twice without, this year.'

'Has he been anywhere else?'

'No, sir. We haven't been able to find out much about his movements in Paris. I've asked M. Ruhamel to cover that.'

71

'Do you know where Mortimer stayed in Paris?'

'His family believed he stayed with friends.'

Every end a dead end, thought Dawlish glumly. He held on for several seconds, but could not think of nothing else useful to say; he was wasting not only his own but also Carruther's time.

'All right,' he said at last. 'Don't miss a trick, this case is . . .'

'Hold on a moment!' Carruthers exclaimed, and there was a clatter as he put the telephone down, followed by a noise in the distance suggesting that he was talking on another line. Dawlish's heart began to beat faster. The younger man wasn't given to excitements.

The door opened, and Ruhamel stepped in. His eyes were glowing as if he were excited, too.

'M. Dawlish . . .'

'We've had a break!' cried Carruthers. 'The Security people have discovered Mortimer's Paris address.'

'M. Dawlish, we know where we can find Mortimer!' cried Ruhamel.

'He goes to 48, Rue Cabot,' Carruthers declared. 'Got that?'

'In the Rue Cabot.' Ruhamel was striding towards the desk.

'How did you get it?' Dawlish asked into the telephone.

'Mrs. Smithers,' Carruthers stated. 'How soon can you get there?'

'I don't know,' Dawlish said. 'Keep it to yourself, don't let anyone who doesn't already know have it. I'll call you back.' He put down the receiver as Ruhamel stood in front of him, eyes blazing with excitement.

It's too easy, he thought. There must be a catch.

'The whole area is being surrounded,' cried Ruhamel, 'and all approaches to Rue Cabot. But we do not want Mortimer to know he has been found. Photographs have reached us, and he was identified by one of our agents, who saw him enter this house only half an hour ago.'

'Wonderful!' Dawlish exclaimed. 'Wonderful!' But he was still thinking: There's a catch, there must be a catch.

'Will you go yourself?' demanded Ruhamel.

There wasn't any choice; and even if there were, there

was only one course open as far as he was concerned.

'Yes.'

'A car is at your disposal, and ...'

'No car,' said Dawlish. 'A taxi.' He was trying to think clearly, trying to prevent Ruhamel from thinking he was taking all this too calmly. 'If I go by car, if I let Mortimer know there are police with me, he might'—cast a shadow, he thought—'open a door,' he said. 'Where is Rue Cabot?'

'Near the Porte d'Orléans.'

'Can I go by Métro?'

'But M. Dawlish ...' Ruhamel's calm was completely broken. 'In view of the emergency ...'

'I can take a radio transmitter,' said Dawlish. 'You can have my movements checked, and the moment anything goes wrong you can take action, but I insist on going by myself. If I do, I might stop Mortimer from opening another door.'

Ruhamel spoke more calmly. 'It is possible. It is also possible that it will be opened especially for you. It that what you think, M. Dawlish? You might attract the danger to yourself?'

'I don't know what I think,' said Dawlish, springing to his feet. 'I simply want to try to find this man myself.'

*   *   *

Leaving the police building, Dawlish strode towards the river. He could get a Métro for the Porte d'Orléans from a station near the Louvre, only ten minutes' walk away. Late though it was, there was traffic and even a few pedestrians. The floodlighting made the main buildings of the Louvre look ghostly, and cast strange shadows. Light and shadows reflected on the unruffled surface of the Seine; boats on the far side of the river caused darker shadows.

No one followed him.

In his pocket was a tiny transmitter, emitting on its own special wavelength; the police could pick him up anywhere.

The stars were very bright.

Strange, the coincidence that both Carruthers and

Ruhamel had told him of Mortimer's address at the same time. Was it possible that Mortimer had meant him to find out?

And if so, why?

To lure him here and kill him? Mortimer would surely have the sense to know that would serve no purpose.

Then—why?

To talk to him?

Dawlish turned down the steps of the Métro station, got some tokens from a machine, and passed through the barrier. A dozen tired-looking people, mostly elderly, were waiting on the platform. The brightly lit tube and the garish advertisements all had an unreal appearance. No one appeared to take any notice of him, either on the platform or when he stepped into the train. Only four other people were in his carriage, and after a lightning glance at each through lowered lashes he leant back and studied a street plan given to him by Ruhamel, memorising the route to Rue Cabot.

Ten minutes later he was going up the station steps and into the street. It was much darker here than in the heart of Paris, but at least two cafés were open. He crossed the road and turned left, checked the name of the first street he passed, then the next, and soon found himself at the end of another. In white on the blue name plaque were the words: Rue Cabot. A dim wall-lamp shone near by.

The first number he saw was 4. He began to walk slowly towards the other end of the street, which seemed filled with shadows.

11

48, RUE CABOT

The houses varied in height and breadth. Some had courtyards in which dim lights glowed, others were shuttered in darkness. Light streamed from one first-floor window, and shadows moved against it; that was No. 32. Two girls, standing on one side, stepped forward into his path.

'M'sieu?'

'*Bonsoir, m'sieu ...*'

'No,' Dawlish said in English. 'No, thank you.'

They drew back.

He was aware of them as he approached No. 48, where another wall-light shone. This was one of the smaller houses, with cracks of light showing at the shuttered windows and at the door. The girls were shadowy figures now, but he sensed that they were watching him. Were they what they seemed or were they associated with Mortimer?

He saw two other girls, further along, also watching. Well, what was surprising about that? Since the new laws on prostitution, one came upon little pockets of it in various places. And it was always possible Ruhamel might be using women agents.

He turned into the doorway of No. 48, just able to see a bell-push. He pressed it, and heard a faint ringing, followed immediately by footsteps. There was something strange about the way these shuffled, as if a very old man or old woman was coming.

Dawlish stood back, prepared almost for anything, acutely aware of the two pairs of watching girls. There was a sound of the door handle turning, then the door creaked open and a misty light shone through the gap, which widened very slowly. Dawlish heard a curious snuffling sound, more like the breath of an animal than that of a human being. *Was* it an animal? he wondered.

The door, three-quarters open, stopped moving. The

sound of breathing came more loudly, but no shape appeared.

'I want to see M. Mortimer,' Dawlish said into the darkness.

There was no reply, but at last the figure of a little boy emerged from behind the door. Dawlish hesitated, and a woman's voice cut across the sound of the boy's strange breathing.

'Who is it, Pierre? Why don't you let him in?'

The boy made a guttural sound, and almost at once a woman appeared from the side of a narrow staircase. Dawlish had the impression of a harassed, young-looking woman, attractive but unkempt, with a tall, slender figure.

'Is M. Mortimer here?' he asked.

'Mortimer?' She put her hands to her hair, tidying it instinctively. 'I know no one of that name.' Her English was good, although the 'that' sounded almost like 'zat'. At closer quarters, he could see that she wasn't made up, that she had sharp but attractive features, dark hair, and dark eyes. 'Do you wish for a room?'

'I was told a Mr. Mortimer would be here.'

'I have t'ree men in the house only—just one an Englishman,' she told him.

'Is he in?'

'If you forgive me, m'sieu, that is his affair.'

'Did he arrive today?' Dawlish asked.

'I do not know when he comes or when he goes.' The woman laid a hand on the boy's shoulder. 'You may go, Pierre,' she said gently. 'You have been very good.'

Pierre turned, and Dawlish saw his face.

It would have shocked him ordinarily, but tonight it came with double impact. It was the face of a cretin; and it was uncannily like the face of Jonah Cotton.

*   *   *

Dawlish watched Pierre shuffle out of sight, then, turning swiftly, saw that the woman had been watching the child also. As she moved back into the passage, he thought her eyes and her expression were the saddest he had ever seen.

'So you do not wish for a room,' she said, in a tone of resignation.

'I want to see ...' Dawlish began, and then he changed his mind quickly. 'Yes, please, I would like a room. Will you show me one?'

Her eyes brightened.

'Follow, please,' she said, and turning on her heel she led Dawlish up a narrow, winding staircase. There was a smell of carbolic, not strong enough to be unpleasant, and at the first landing a single light glowed. Nodding towards it, she turned up the next flight of stairs.

'The girls live there.'

Ah! thought Dawlish.

'There are two floors above, one for a family apartment —do you wish for more than one room?'

'No.'

'Then I will show you the only single room I have to offer.'

Arriving at the second landing, she reached for a large, old-fashioned key which Dawlish had noticed dangling from the belt of her dress. Following her past an open door, he glimpsed a W.C. with a high cistern and long chain; the cistern hissed and gurgled. Next to this was a closed door marked *'Bain'*; and next, another closed door, which the woman unlocked.

She switched on a light, brighter than those in the rest of the house, and motioned Dawlish into the room. It was large and bleak. In one corner was a heavy iron bedstead, and beside it, an upright wooden chair. A wardrobe stood against the opposite wall, and there was a square of shabby carpet on the worn linoleum which covered the floor.

'This is all I have,' she said flatly.

'How much?'

'Twenty-five francs a week. But you must pay in advance, please.'

'Will English money do?'

'It will be two pounds in English money.'

'Thank you.' Dawlish took two pounds from his wallet, and gave them to her. 'May I have a key?'

'This one, yes. Pierre or I will unlock the front door. Have you any luggage?'

77

'It will come later.'

The woman nodded, and now, in the brighter light, Dawlish saw that her eyes were large and beautiful, but very tired, with dark patches beneath them.

'I hope you will not be disturbed,' she said.

'Who would disturb me?' Dawlish inquired.

She shrugged. 'The girls sometimes bring a man who is drunk.'

'That won't worry me. What is your name?' Dawlish asked. 'Madame . . .?'

'*Mam'selle* Blanc. There is a café at the corner, if you turn right out of the front door,' she added, speaking as if to dispel any impression of bitterness her emphasis on the word 'mam'selle' may have created. 'You can get good bread and good croissants there. And the coffee is not so bad.'

'Thank you, mam'selle, thank you indeed. I will do that.' Dawlish's voice was gentle.

'Good night, m'sieu.'

'Good night, mam'selle'—Dawlish followed her to the doorway—'what is the name of your English guest?'

She turned to face him. 'Is it of importance, m'sieu?'

'If he is the man I think he is, it could be very important.'

Deliberately, she said: 'He calls himself Miller.' She made the name sound like 'Millair'—and she said 'he calls himself' as if to imply that he was obviously using a false name. 'Will you please answer me one question?'

'If I can.'

'Are you from the police?'

Was there any point in lying? If this was a false trail then it did not matter what Mademoiselle Blanc knew; if Miller *was* Mortimer, Dawlish would reveal himself for what he was immediately.

'Yes, I am a kind of policeman,' he said. 'Do you expect the police to be interested in M. Miller?'

'I expect nothing,' she said. 'I like to know who is living here. Good night, M'sieu Dawlish.'

She nodded, and went out, closing the door behind her.

Dawlish waited for a few moments, then, turning the handle as quietly as he was able, opened the door a few inches and peered outside. The landing was empty. Stealthily, he crossed to the door opposite his. The card in the bracket under the brass knocker read 'Pannier', and he moved quickly to the next door. This was marked 'Miller.'

As he examined the lock, Dawlish found himself wondering why Mortimer should select such a place as a hideout, and he began seriously to wonder whether Mortimer *was* Miller; whether, in fact, the physicist had ever set foot in No. 48, Rue Cabot.

He forced the lock nevertheless, paused, then opened the door an inch, seeing only darkness beyond. There was no sound. Yet he hesitated. If this was Mortimer's room, then there was no certainty that the ingot was not inside, its container partly open.

Don't be a damn fool! he exhorted himself. If it were, I'd be a heap of ashes already.

He pushed the door wider open, and switched on the light.

On the bed a man, who looked exactly like the photographs he had seen of Mortimer, lay and stared at him.

Dawlish stood motionless, his finger still on the light switch. From below came voices and a bellow of laughter, followed by the slamming of a door. The laughter and voices remained audible, but seemed further away. Dawlish closed the door and leaned on it.

'Mortimer alias Miller?' he asked.

'Yes, I answer to both,' said Eric Mortimer. 'This is quite a distinction—to have a visit from such a highly placed officer from Scotland Yard. How did you find me, Mr. Dawlish?'

'We followed the trail you left deliberately,' said Dawlish.

'Why on earth should I leave a deliberate trail?' Mortimer hitched himself up on his elbows. This room was much better furnished, and the bed and bedclothes were of far superior quality to those in the other room.

'Presumably, so that you could talk to me,' Dawlish said. 'Now that I'm here, where is the ingot?'

Mortimer lay back on the pillows. 'In a safe place.'

'I want it.'

'Don't be a fool,' said Mortimer.

'You're the fool, thinking you can get away with this,' Dawlish countered.

'I *am* getting away with it,' declared Mortimer.

'No,' answered Dawlish. 'You just think you are. So far, you seem to have killed one man, one old woman, and two dogs.' He knew that there might be many more victims of the shadow in the Rue des Rennes but let the thought pass. 'Why don't you stop before you've gone too far?'

'I don't want to stop,' said Mortimer. 'And even if I did, I couldn't.'

'What's to prevent you?'

'My—colleagues.'

'Your bosses, you mean.'

'I mean what I say—my colleagues.' Mortimer sat up and a cigarette from a packet on a bedside table. 'We have the ultimate weapon, Dawlish.'

'Ultimate weapons, one, stolen, mankind for the use of,' said Dawlish woodenly. 'Likely to be out-of-date at any time.'

'Not this one,' Mortimer said. 'There can't ever be enough absolute protection against this one. It would take too long and be too costly to develop.'

Dawlish didn't answer.

'My friend,' Mortimer went on, 'anyone who possesses this weapon can spread human destruction wherever he wishes. How much would you say it's worth?'

'It hasn't a value,' Dawlish answered.

'Ten million pounds, perhaps?' Mortimer suggested.

Dawlish drew in his breath sharply, and Mortimer let smoke drift from his lips and curl about his head. It added a strange touch of unreality to the scene.

'So it's money you want,' said Dawlish heavily.

'That's it,' Mortimer admitted. 'Money. And because I'm an Englishman I would rather sell this weapon to Britain or one of her allies than to the Chinese or the Russians. Ten million pounds isn't really expensive when you realise how much damage it can do. I'm ready to talk terms, Dawlish—on behalf of my colleagues.' He hitched himself up again, and stubbed the cigarette out on an ashtray. 'But the offer won't last for ever. Only for twenty-four hours, in fact.'

He smiled—and there was something likeable about his appearance, a touch almost of gaiety. It was easy to imagine how he could appeal to women. For the first time since he had come here, Dawlish thought of Wanda Hordle, who had died believing she was opening the door to this man.

'How do you know I haven't a cordon flung round this place, so that whatever happens you can't benefit from ten pounds, never mind ten million?'

Mortimer chuckled.

'I know,' he said. 'The girls who rent the rooms here come from all over this part of Paris—and they would have warned me. When the girl came in with her new friend just now, she was telling me the street was clear. You came alone, to talk business, Dawlish—and I'm talking business. Ten million pounds is the sum demanded. Ten caches of one million each are to be placed at our disposal in ten different places.' When Dawlish made no comment, Mortimer went on with a laugh: 'One each in London, Paris, Rome, Brussels, New York, Tokyo, Buenos Aires, New Delhi, Cairo, and Mexico City. You see how wide our net is spread. When the principle of this has been accepted, you will be told how the money must be paid over.'

His tone was so light-hearted, he might have been talking about tickets for a show. He paused only for a few moments, then sprang lightly off the bed.

'It really is cheap at the price,' he said. 'Go and tell your masters, Dawlish, and hurry back!'

He was absolutely sure of himself, sure that Dawlish would have to do what he said. But Dawlish did not move, just stood with his back to the door and studied the other man, whose smile began to fade, and whose voice suddenly became strident.

'Get going,' he ordered. 'You haven't any time to spare.'

'You haven't any time at all,' Dawlish told him quietly. 'Unless you tell me where the ingot is, I'm going to kill you with my bare hands.'

For the first time, he took a step forward.

81

And for the first time, Eric Mortimer seemed to be afraid.

Dawlish took another step forward, and Mortimer thrust his hand under the pillows and snatched out a gun.

12

MAN OF STRAW

The gun, small and squat, was dark and menacing against the whiteness of Mortimer's hand. Dawlish was two yards away, the gun pointing at his face—one shot could kill him. He stood absolutely still, like an enormous statue.

'That's—that's better,' gasped Mortimer. 'Get back, or I'll kill you. I don't care who I deal with. If you die, someone will replace you.'

'You cold-blooded swine,' grated Dawlish.

On the last word he flung himself forward, dropping to his knees as he did so. There was the roar of a shot, but the bullet passed harmlessly over his head and he clutched Mortimer's ankles, and tugged. The man toppled over helplessly, another shot rang out and a bullet buried itself in the floor only inches from Dawlish's head. The gun was still held in Mortimer's hand, but loosely. Dawlish, springing to his feet, took the man's wrist and twisted savagely.

Mortimer screamed, and the gun dropped.

Footsteps thudded up the stairs.

Dawlish swung a blow at Mortimer's jaw, sent the man reeling against the bed, swung round and turned the key in the lock, then grabbed a chair and jammed it beneath the handle. Almost simultaneously, a man thudded against the door from the outside, and a woman called out in French:

'Be careful!'

Mortimer was half off the bed, half on it. His lips were

quivering, his eyes glassy with fear. The floor shook as the man outside hurled himself against it again.

'Stop that and go away,' called Dawlish. 'If you don't, then I'll break this man's neck.'

'No!' gasped Mortimer. 'No!'

'Tell him to go away,' Dawlish ordered. 'Tell him to stop.'

Mortimer gasped out orders in fluent French. The stranger outside grumbled, but seemed compliant. Dawlish moved the chair swiftly, unbolted the door—and saw a large, broad-shouldered man, his lips parted in surprise. Behind him was a girl with blonde hair over naked shoulders, a towel round her waist, behind her were two more girls and, at the head of the stairs, Mademoiselle Blanc.

Dawlish drove his fist with tremendous force into the man's stomach, and the stranger staggered back and collapsed against the wall, trying desperately to get his breath.

One of the girls turned and fled towards the stairs.

'Stop!' roared Dawlish, and the girl stopped in midflight. 'Mam'selle Blanc, listen to me,' he went on in a calm, quiet voice. 'Lock the front and back doors and let no one in or out of the house. Make sure all the windows are shuttered. If you don't, I shall have the police sent for and you will be accused of keeping a brothel. Do you understand me?'

Mademoiselle Blanc stood without moving; how weary she looked, Dawlish thought in a moment of compassion, how hopeless. But before she could answer him, a sound came from behind her: a whimpering; then a shuffling. It was Pierre, rounding a curve in the stairs, tears streaming down his face.

'Hurry,' Dawlish made himself say.

As he spoke, he saw a sudden change of expression in Mademoiselle Blanc's eyes, heard a faint creak, and knew that Mortimer was creeping up behind him. Swinging round, he saw Mortimer with a chair half-raised, ready to crash down on his head. Thrusting out his leg, he jabbed Mortimer with his foot. Mortimer went reeling backwards, the chair fell, and there was a splintering of wood as it crashed to the floor.

Mademoiselle Blanc turned to the girls. 'You will go to your rooms,' she said quietly. Then she glanced at Dawlish, nodded, and shepherded the girls down the stairs, Pierre clutching her arm.

Dawlish crossed the landing to the stranger, who had slumped to the floor, still gasping for breath. Seizing his ankles, he dragged him into the empty, windowless bathroom, took the key from the inside, and locked the door on him. Then he went back to Mortimer, who was trying to get to his feet, in the doorway of his own room. Dawlish took his right wrist and dragged him inside, closed but did not lock the door, and let the man go.

'You—you don't know what you're doing,' Mortimer muttered.

'I know exactly what I'm doing,' said Dawlish. 'I'm making sure you don't benefit from any of that ten million. Unless you've found a way of getting money through to the next world.'

'You wouldn't kill me!'

'You think not?' asked Dawlish gently, his very gentleness making his words the more menacing. 'You really think not?' Suddenly his tone changed. 'Where's the ingot?' he barked.

'I—I don't know!'

'A pity,' said Dawlish, mildly. 'That was your only chance of staying alive.'

'No!' gasped Mortimer. 'No!'

Dawlish stretched out his hands and closed them round Mortimer's neck. Mortimer clutched at his captor's wrists, trying to scratch, but making no mark at all. Slowly, remorselessly, Dawlish tightened his grasp until Mortimer could no longer draw breath. The terror in his eyes began to fade as unconsciousness came.

His head flopped to one side.

Dawlish let him go, then turned him over on his stomach, quite gently, knelt astride him and applied artificial respiration. Directly he heard a rasping intake of breath, he climbed free. For the first time since he had entered this house, he felt that he dared relax.

Dropping on to the foot of the bed, he leaned against

the wall, drawing a hand across his forehead; it was dripping with sweat.

Seeing a hand-basin in the room, he made himself get up and go across to it, ran cold water, filled his cupped hands, and doused his face. Then he turned back to Mortimer.

The man was breathing more easily now, and Dawlish rolled him over on to his back. 'Next time, you won't come round. Understand?'

Mortimer's eyes fluttered open, and he tried to nod.

'You're only useful alive if you can lead me to the ingot,' Dawlish went on. 'It won't help if you lead me on a false trail, either—I would kill you afterwards.'

'You—you're a policeman!' muttered Mortimer.

'That's right. A policeman who will kill you and a dozen others to prevent you using the ingot again. When it's a few lives against millions, I don't work by the rules. Sit up.'

'I—I can't move.'

'*Sit up!*' Dawlish roared.

Slowly, laboriously, Mortimer struggled to a sitting position.

'Where's the ingot?' Dawlish demanded.

Mortimer drew in a hissing breath.

'I don't know, I swear I don't know! I only had to deliver it to—to the others, then—then talk to you.'

'So you made sure the police knew where to find you.'

'Yes—I—*they* did!'

'Who are *they*?'

'My—my colleagues.'

'Name them.'

'One—one is Bruckner,' Mortimer said hoarsely. 'The other is Svenson.'

'A German and a Swede?'

'I—I think so.'

'Who do they work for?'

'Them—themselves.' As Dawlish bent towards him, Mortimer shrank back and thrust his arms outwards, but it was like trying to fend off an elephant with pieces of straw. 'That's all I know, I've always worked for them.'

'Ah,' said Dawlish. 'How long is always?'

'Two—two years or so.'

'Two? Or three or four . . .'

'Just over two. That's all, I swear it is. I—I was over here for a weekend, they came to see me, they—they offered me a partnership.'

'You pass on secrets from the Research Establishment, and they pay you. Is that it?'

'They—they were only industrial secrets, that's all, they weren't security risks.'

'Poor Britain,' said Dawlish, 'to have traitors like you.' He stared into Mortimer's eyes. 'I'm not interested in what you've done in the past except where it affects what you're doing now. What do you know about these men?'

'They—they're partners, they've got business contacts, they get good prices for—for industrial know-how. I haven't told them much, the Midlands Research Establishment hasn't been going for long, there hasn't been much in it for me.'

Dawlish managed to keep the cold anger out of his voice.

'Did you always meet here?'

'Yes.'

'Who owns the house?'

'I—I don't know his name, or who he is, but it's someone who works with Bruckner and Svensen.'

'What about the girls?' demanded Dawlish. 'Do *they* work with Bruckner and Svensen?'

'They—they give us preference. If—if none of the agents—the contact men . . .'

'If they're not wanted by you or other agents they can bring home who they like. Is that it?'

'Yes,' muttered Mortimer.

'Did you know that your—your *colleagues*—were going to kill Wanda?'

Mortimer, lips and hands unsteady until that moment, went suddenly still. At first, Dawlish thought it was a trick. Then, seeing the colour drain from the man's face, he realised that it was genuine shock.

Mortimer's voice came from the back of his throat, in a hoarse whisper.

'They wouldn't—kill her!'

86

'They killed her in cold blood.'

'You're—you're lying to me!'

'I went to see her,' Dawlish said flatly. 'There was a ring at the door, a little before she expected you. She thought it *was* you. She went to the door and a man stabbed her to the heart. She died instantaneously.'

Mortimer's forehead was covered with beads of sweat which were growing bigger. One trickled down into his left eye. Dawlish took out his wallet and selected a photograph of Wanda which had been taken at the flat in St. John's Wood. He held it out but Mortimer made no attempt to touch it, just stared down.

His lips quivered.

'I can't believe it.'

'She was murdered. You knew it was going to happen—just as you knew about Mrs. Smithers.'

Mortimer said, whispering: 'I didn't know. Oh, God. Wanda! I swear I didn't know.'

'Mrs. Smithers—remember her?' asked Dawlish.

Mortimer looked blank. 'Who?'

'Mrs. Smithers.'

'Who's she?'

'Major Hordle's housekeeper.'

'Oh, *her*.'

'You told her to spy on Major Hordle, remember.'

Mortimer seemed to make a great effort to pull himself together, and his voice grew stronger.

'I did nothing of the kind.'

'Mortimer,' said Dawlish quietly, 'Mrs. Smithers told me that *you* had arranged for her to go down to Devon and find out whether Wanda had told her father anything which might betray you. I don't believe ...'

'My God!' cried Mortimer. 'I'll kill them. I'll kill them with my bare hands. The swine, they ...' He was gasping with rage. 'They asked me if I was sure she wouldn't say anything. I laughed at them, because she didn't *know* anything, I'd never said a word to her about it. My God!' He caught his breath, then stumbled clumsily to his feet. 'I'll choke the life out of them!'

'So you do know where to find them,' said Dawlish slowly.

87

13

SHOP OF ANTIQUES

Again, Mortimer caught his breath.

Dawlish, three-quarters convinced that the outburst of passion had been genuine, watched closely as the expression in his eyes changed. He realised he had given himself away, of course. Would he try to bluff it out, or would he now co-operate?

Still tense, still hoarse-voiced, he said: 'They've an apartment on the left bank—in the Rue des Saints Pères.'

'What number?'

'Two hundred and seven. Dawlish, I swear to you I'll kill them with my bare hands!' For the first time Mortimer picked up the photograph and held it close. 'To kill *her*.'

'You can leave them to me,' Dawlish said quietly.

'No! No, *I* want to deal with them. This is my job, Dawlish.'

Dawlish shook his head. 'If you go first you'll either try to kill them or you'll warn them to expect me. Forget it!'

'Dawlish, you don't understand—I loved Wanda!'

Mortimer was almost choking, but this did not stop him from springing towards the door. Taken by surprise. Dawlish grabbed at him, caught his sleeve, then lost his grip. At the same moment Mortimer back-heeled, striking Dawlish on the shin. The pain was momentarily agonising, and Dawlish caught his breath and staggered on one leg.

Mortimer opened the door and rushed outside.

As Dawlish recovered the door slammed. As he reached and grabbed the handle, he heard the man clattering down the stairs, then heard him roar:

'Get out of my way!'

Dawlish pulled the door open, snatching up the broken chair as he did so, and bounded to the head of the stairs.

Mortimer was halfway down.

'Get that child out of my way!' he was screaming.

Dawlish looked past him, to Pierre, huddled at the foot of the stairs, and Mademoiselle Blanc behind him.

'Get him out of the way!' screeched Mortimer.

Then he jumped.

The terror-stricken boy crouched, big hands near his chin, mouth wide open. The woman snatched at his shoulder but he was far too heavy to be pulled aside.

Dawlish hurled the chair at Mortimer's back. Mortimer staggered helplessly, the boy set up a series of ear-piercing shrieks and the woman took him into her arms, soothing him in a tense and frantic way. As Mortimer tried to recover his balance, Dawlish reached him, gripping him by the shoulders and shaking him so violently that his head bobbed to and fro as if his neck were broken.

The boy's screaming slackened.

The woman stared at Dawlish, open-mouthed.

'Stop, please stop,' she pleaded at last. 'You'll kill him. Please stop.' There was entreaty in her eyes.

Dawlish released his hold, and Mortimer flopped over the banister rail. Perhaps he *had* broken the man's neck, thought Dawlish. Hoisting the inert body over his shoulder, he carried Mortimer upstairs, dropped him on the bed, and felt his pulse. It was still beating.

Running through Mortimer's pockets, he transferred some loose papers and a bunch of keys to his own. Then he pulled a sheet off the bed, tore it in two, knotted the ends to make a rope, and bound the man to the bed. Crossing to the bedroom door, he took the key from the lock and locked the door from the outside. Then he ran down the two flights of stairs to the ground floor.

Mademoiselle Blanc and Pierre were still where he had left them.

'He's alive,' said Dawlish.

'Thank God!'

'You like him?' Dawlish demanded.

'I do not want you to be a murderer,' she said quietly.

'Thank you, mam'selle. And I do not want you, or others, to be hurt. Mortimer is tied to his bed—please do not release him. The other man is locked in the bathroom, and should soon start trying to get out. Let him go. If he threatens you, tell him I'll be back, with the police, at any moment.'

'I will do what you say.'

'Where are the girls?'

'They will be in their rooms.'

'Make sure they don't go out again tonight,' said Dawlish. 'Give them what you think they will lose.' He put six English five-pound notes into her hands, and she took them as if unbelievingly.

'Will you—will you come back?' Her voice was husky.

'I shall try to.'

'In the name of myself and my son—God be with you.'

She crossed herself.

Dawlish pressed her shoulder gently, and then went out. He paused at the door but this time saw no one in the street: no girls huddled in a doorway, only the shadows and the dim lights. A car passed the far end of the street, then another. There might be a taxi near the Métro station. He stepped out, feeling pain at one knee and in his left shoulder, but not enough to impede him. The night was cool, almost cold. His neck and waist and forehead felt clammy, and suddenly he shivered. As he turned into the lighted thoroughfare, an *agent de police* and a plain-clothes man appeared from a doorway and came towards him. A man sat on the kerb, his head between his knees; another lay huddled in a doorway.

The agent spoke sharply. 'Your identity card, if you please, m'sieu.'

Dawlish hesitated. He did not want to be followed, did not want the slightest risk of warning Bruckner and Svensen, who might still be at 207, Rue des Saints Pères.

He could run . . .

But the police would almost certainly catch up with him and he might lose precious hours. If he confided in them, however, and they helped him to get to the Rue des Saints Pères, word might be sent ahead to Svensen and Bruckner. Any one of the derelict men, any girl on the streets, anyone at a window, might be watching him.

'I have my passport,' he said, and took it out.

The agent examined it, flicking over the pages, and speaking in a low voice as he did so.

'We know who you are, M'sieu Dawlish. We are to

assist you in any way possible without arousing attention. Is there anything we can do?'

Dawlish's heart began to beat faster.

'If I turn right, and keep walking fast, can you have a taxi follow me? One I can hire.'

'Yes, of course.'

'Thanks. Have a watch kept on the Rue des Saints Pères —and the whole area.'

'I will arrange it, m'sieu.' The man closed the passport and handed it back. 'That is the area of L'École des Beaux Arts, and also of St. Germain de Près. It is easy to get lost there.'

'Yes,' said Dawlish.

'Do you wish for help?'

'Only if I send for it,' Dawlish said. 'I want to go alone —and no one should be sent there until I have arrived.'

'I understand m'sieu. What if anyone leaves the house in the Rue Cabot?'

'Have their movements watched but don't pick them up.'

'Very good.' The agent gave a casual salute, and turned away with his companion.

Dawlish walked with long deliberate strides along the boulevard, turning his head every now and again, hoping to see a taxi. There was none in sight, and after a few minutes he began to wonder whether he had been deceived. Then a taxi appeared, a sleek, modern Citroën with its beak-like bonnet. He waved and the driver pulled in.

'M'sieu?'

'Two hundred and seven Rue des Saints Pères.'

'*Oui, m'sieu.*'

The boulevard was almost deserted, as all the streets would be at this hour, but even bowling along at seventy or eighty kilometres an hour, it would take twenty minutes to reach the house where he might find Svensen and Bruckner. Dawlish leaned back and closed his eyes; the lids felt like leaden weights. He needed sleep badly, but he forced himself to concentrate, warning himself that he had no proof that Bruckner and Svensen even existed. Mortimer might have fooled him utterly. Judging by appearances, however, Dawlish was pretty certain he hadn't known about the murder of Wanda Hordle.

And if he had told the truth and he hadn't given Mrs. Smithers any instructions, this meant that she had lied.

He, Dawlish, had already told Childs to investigate the woman's past and her associations, so there was nothing more to be done. What a contrast—Mrs. Smithers with a pleasant and comfortable job in Devonshire, Mademoiselle Blanc acting like a brothel-keeper in a back street of Paris. Why did a woman of her calibre live in such a way? Why had she emphasised the fact that she wasn't married, and that Pierre was her son? It was almost as if she were flagellating herself by not allowing herself to forget the lapse which had caused such tragedy.

Lapse?

Perhaps the father had promised marriage ...

Dawlish sat up and made himself think about Jonah Cotton. There, but for the grace of God and a few chemical differences, went another Pierre. What a narrow margin separated a woman from a happy marriage and a pride in her children on the one hand—from shame and misery on the other.

Ahead, Dawlish glimpsed the soaring outline of the Eiffel Tower against the starlit sky. So they were drawing near. Lights shone on the gilded eagles at the end of the bridge leading from the Palace Royale. He straightened up again. What he really needed was food; he felt ravenous, and was only just beginning to realise it.

The taxi took a turning to the right, seemed to lose itself, then swung left out of a narrow side street—and on a wall plaque, Dawlish read: Rue des Saints Pères; a shop doorway carried the number 71. The taxi began to slow down, and soon stopped. Dawlish got out.

'How much?'

'Six francs, m'sieu.'

Dawlish paid fifteen, and heard the driver's warm *'Merci beaucoup, m'sieu, merci beaucoup.'* It was an achievement to have moved a French cabby to enthusiasm. The taxi moved off, and Dawlish stood alone in the narrow, deserted street, then began to walk slowly towards No. 207.

He had never known Paris so still, so silent.

It was almost as if a dark shadow had been cast over the city. A dark shadow . . .

Nonsense, he was letting his imagination run away with him, Dawlish told himself. The night was clear and the air was brisk, and Mortimer had almost certainly told the truth. He drew close to No. 207. It was a shop, with a few heavy, ugly-looking antiques in a single window, and some faded prints in one corner. There was no name on the window or the fascia.

Dawlish tried the shop door, finding, as he had expected, that it was locked. Taking out his pick-lock, he slipped it into the key-hole, twisted it, and felt it catch almost immediately. The door was still held at the top, obviously by a bolt, but it was ill-fitting, and he was able to insert a blade of his knife between the door and the jamb, and gradually ease the bolt back.

The door opened.

He stepped inside, closing and locking it behind him. The stillness outside had been noticeable enough: here it was even more so, the impression heightened by the fusty smell, as if the dust and creeping dampness of years lay in this shop.

A car turned into the street.

Dawlish heard it approaching, then saw the beam of its headlights through the window. The engine was very noisy, and he thought the car was about to stop. Could this be the police? Or one of the two men he had come to see? He stood behind a huge wardrobe as the car stopped immediately outside. The door opened and slammed, the footsteps of a woman came sharp and clear on the pavement—then she began to bang against the glass of the shop door.

Dawlish could just make out her face in the dim street light.

It was Mademoiselle Blanc.

14

THE MESSAGE

She kept up a continuous banging and rattling of the door, calling out something which Dawlish could not hear. She did not appear to mind how much attention she attracted, so there was obviously nothing secret about her visit—but why had she come?

Dawlish heard no sound from above.

He stepped into sight, suddenly, and the woman saw him and stood motionless, her hand raised in the act of striking the glass of the door yet again. At the same moment a man appeared behind her, elderly-looking and frail. She glanced round but was not alarmed.

No one's upstairs, thought Dawlish, or this racket would have made them move.

He opened the door.

'You—you are *safe!*' gasped Mademoiselle Blanc.

'Why shouldn't I be safe?' demanded Dawlish.

She made no attempt to answer at first, she was struggling so desperately to regain her breath. The old man looked up at Dawlish through shaggy eyebrows, but did not speak. Parked at the kerb was a very old Renault, with the sign *Taxi* showing on the roof.

'Why shouldn't I be safe?' repeated Dawlish.

Her eyes looked enormous as she stared at him.

'There was a—message for M. Miller.'

Miller? thought Dawlish. Oh—Miller alias Mortimer.

'What message?' he asked.

'He was told not to come here, or he would be killed.' She caught her breath again, then in a sharp voice spoke to the old man. 'Why do you stand there? Return to the car and wait for me.'

She glared at him, and he looked at her like a dog which had been scolded for no reason, and turned back to the taxi.

'Come in,' said Dawlish.

She started back. 'No!'

'Why not?'

'The message said—he must not go in or he would die.'

'I'm in, and I've come to no harm.'

'Please,' she entreated. 'Please come away.'

Dawlish did not move.

'Did the message say how Miller would be killed?' he asked.

'There was some danger from—from a box.'

'*Box!*'

'That is what the message said,' Mademoiselle Blanc insisted. 'Please do not stay here.'

'How did you get the message?' Dawlish demanded.

'There was a telephone call, but I could not bring M. Miller down to speak. I asked for the message, and the man ...'

'Man?'

'Yes. A German, I think, to judge from his voice. He said the box was here, at 207, Rue des Saints Pères. I went upstairs to Miller. I made him tell me what this meant. He told me that you had come here—that *you* would be in danger.'

'*Mortimer* did,' breathed Dawlish.

'M. Miller said you were here, and if you came inside you would die.'

'But I'm not dead,' said Dawlish quietly.

'M'sieu, *please* ...'

Dawlish took her arm, and spoke in a low-pitched voice.

'I know what he meant, but I have to go upstairs. There is danger, but there is no need for you to suffer from it. Go back to the Rue Cabot. Go back, and wait.'

'But m'sieu ...'

Dawlish led her firmly towards the taxi, and the old man climbed out of the driver's seat and opened the rear door.

'Turn round and go back,' Dawlish ordered.

'But, m'sieu ...'

'Do what I tell you!' roared Dawlish. 'Turn round ...'

'It is a one-way street, m'sieu!' wailed the old man.

'Do what I tell you,' said Dawlish again. 'And when you come to a telephone, call the Sûreté Nationale and ask for M. Ruhamel. You have that name?'

'M. Ruhamel, m'sieu.'

'That right. Tell him of the message, tell him that I'm here.'

Ruhamel would have the whole area cordoned off, of course, would try desperately not to risk more deaths from the shadow. Dawlish closed the taxi door, and turned back towards the shop. Few people could live about here or someone would have come to investigate the disturbance. The police were co-operating fully, yet he had never felt more alone.

And he had never been more coldly frightened.

Why should anyone warn Mortimer unless there were good cause? Yet whoever it was, could not have known that he, Dawlish, was on his way here; no matter how he tried, Dawlish could not see a plot against him in this. Someone knew the ingot had been left here and had been desperate to keep Mortimer away.

But if the container was closed, then there could be no danger. And it could not be open, thought Dawlish grimly, or that fatal shadow would have caused yet further unspeakable devastation. There was obviously no one here to open it—where, then, was the danger? he wondered.

Could the container be *blown* open—by a time bomb, perhaps?

If it were, then the shadow would be cast in all directions.

It *did* go through walls. He had seen the evidence. And if anyone was touched by the shadow it *did* reduce them to ashes.

How could he, Dawlish, stop it?

Wasn't it madness even to try?

It would be possible to have the shop surrounded with lead panels but this would take an age. He did not know when the explosion—if his supposition was correct—was timed.

If there were a restricted range it might be justifiable to take a chance, but the range was very wide. Too wide. But there was a way—just one way—to make sure that no harm could come from it. And that was to see the container remained closed.

That was why he was here: to overcome the danger. He had no choice at all.

Dawlish heard the taxi engine growling as the old man put it into bottom gear, and his last glimpse of the street showed the woman's face at the window.

Then he turned towards the back of the shop.

There was a door at one side, and he reached it and touched the handle. The door was unlocked. He stepped into a narrow passage and groped for a light switch. He found it and pressed it down. Light, eerie and bright, showed a passage and a flight of narrow stairs.

There was no sound, no sound at all. Dawlish crept up the stairs, ears strained, hardly daring to breathe. He reached the landing and stood still, then heard a faint tick-tick-tick-tick ...

It could be a clock.

Or it could be the mechanism which would blow that container to pieces.

* * *

On the right of Dawlish were more light switches. Curving round to one side was another flight of stairs. Off the landing were three heavy-looking doors with ornately carved lintels.

The tick-tick-tick-tick became more insistent.

What time was it?

What did that matter? He didn't know what time the infernal machine was to go off.

Tick-tick-tick-tick ...

It was coming from the room ahead. The door wasn't quite closed, and Dawlish could see that the room was in darkness. He tried to make himself hurry but feared that if he set up any vibration he might set the thing off. Cautiously, he edged towards the door, listened for a moment, then pushed it wider open.

The ticking grew louder.

He found another switch and pressed it down.

This light was mellow, and shone about a beautifully furnished room—some modern pieces, some antique, but

97

each chosen with exquisite care. The carpet was azure blue, the chairs and couch, pale green. It was a woman's room rather than a man's, Dawlish thought.

There was a clock, on a marble mantel-shelf.

There was a box, looking rather like a black typewriter case, on a coffee table in the middle of the room.

Dawlish crossed to it. As he reached it his heart gave one convulsive leap, and then steadied. He was acutely aware of the danger but no longer aware of fear. He felt ice cold. During those days when he had dropped behind enemy lines, he had trained in bomb disposal and was not unused to booby trap bombs and mines like this one. Or at least, like this one appeared to be.

Usually, to put them into water was a help.

Why hadn't he found the bathroom and started to fill the bath?

He went down on one knee to examine the box more closely. It almost exactly resembled Cotton's description of the ingot's container, but had one significant difference—it stood on a small, square stand, to which it was securely wired. He put his head against the stand and the ticking was both loud and clear; there was no doubt at all that this stand contained the bomb mechanism.

Dawlish drew in a deep breath and then lifted the box with great care. He glanced at the clock on the mantel-shelf. Was there any reason to believe that it would explode on the hour? If so, he had three minutes. Three minutes. The wire was twisted tightly, and to untwist it he would need pliers. Would the blade on his knife be enough? Quite steadily, he laid the box on the coffee table and took out the knife, selecting the blade required; then, very carefully, he bent over the stand. Dare he use half a minute to find the bathroom and run the bath? No. He had to face facts, and the most important fact was that it made little difference whether or not he was blown to pieces—what did matter was the preservation of the box. As these things passed through his mind, he was working on the wire; the plier-blade did get a grip but it was tediously slow work.

Three minutes would not be enough.

Dawlish moistened his lips, and felt sweat stinging

his forehead.

Now he was vividly aware of two lots of ticking; one from the stand, one from the clock. Slowly, slowly, he uncoiled the twisted wire. One side was undone, the other loose. He placed the stand closer to the edge of the table, so that he would be able to finish the job quicker—and his blade slipped and dug into his left forefinger. He gasped with pain, but hardly stopped. There *could* be only seconds left.

Tick-tick-tick-tick . . .

He heard another sound behind him.

Blood was welling up from his finger, the last coil of the wire was now loose, but he went absolutely rigid. Someone was at the door.

He turned his head slowly.

Mademoiselle Blanc was coming into the room. She stared at him, catching her breath when she saw the blood. Now Dawlish's heart began to beat with heavy thumps. What was she doing here?

'Can I—please can I help?' she pleaded.

Help, thought Dawlish; my God, has she come back for that?

The last coil was free!

She stood very close to him.

'Yes,' he said, drawing the stand away from the container and leaving the container on the table. 'That box is very heavy. Take it in both hands and carry it downstairs. Don't let it fall. Take it as far as you can and then put it on the pavement. And whatever happens, *do not open it.* If I don't come back, send for the police, and tell them I told you to give it to them.'

'If—if you don't come back?' Her voice was anguished.

'Just take it,' Dawlish said. 'Hurry.'

She looked at his bloodied hand. She looked at his sweaty face, grey with strain. She held out her hands and he placed the container deliberately on to them.

'It's very heavy,' he warned her.

Her arms sagged under the weight, but she held the container firmly.

'Don't lose a moment,' Dawlish said.

99

She went across the room like a woman sleep-walking, out by the open door, down the curving staircase. Dawlish heard her slow, deliberate footsteps—heard also that double ticking, one across the other so that now the tick-tick-tick-tick seemed to carry ever greater urgency, as if it were saying: hurry-hurry-hurry-hurry ...

Carefully he lifted the stand, but blood made his hand slippery and he almost dropped it; his heart leapt wildly. Clutching it more tightly, he carried it out of the room, tried the first door which was a bedroom, tried the next and found the bathroom. Placing the stand in the bath, he draped two heavy towels and a towelling wrap over it, then turned on both taps. The towel began to float as the bath filled. Stifling a ridiculous impulse to wait and turn the water off, he swung round and hurried out of the room and down the stairs, expecting at any moment to be blasted off his feet.

He reached the shop and ran towards the door, which now stood wide open. He went out—and as he reached the pavement, heard a muffled roar from the room he had just left. Glass smashed, fragments clattered and tinkled about the pavement and the road, he felt a sharp pain at his forehead, another at the back of his head, but neither was serious.

He had saved the container, thank God. He had saved the container!

Then an absurd thought flashed into his mind: how could he be sure that the ingot was inside it?

15

INGOT?

At last, people stirred.

Windows opened; doors opened; voices were raised. A child began to scream. A man called: 'Fire, fire!'

As Dawlish ran towards the end of the street towards the river, people stared at him and called out: 'Stop him, stop him!' Two police cars turned into the street, headlights blazing, sirens blaring. Just round the corner was a taxi cab and half a dozen policemen—and by the side of the cab stood Mademoiselle Blanc and the old man who had brought her here. The taxi engine was idling noisily, and the old vehicle was shaking as if it would fall to pieces. The police cars drew up and a cordon of police was flung across the end of the Rue des Saints Pères. A uniformed man was talking to the woman rapidly in French.

A man who came up as far as Dawlish's shoulder stood squarely, aggressively, in front of him, revolver drawn. 'Stop there!' Dawlish stopped. 'Who are you?'

Dawlish said with great deliberation: 'I need to see M. Ruhamel at once.'

'M. Ruhamel!'

Another, bigger man in plain clothes came up.

'You are M. Dawlish?'

'Yes.'

'Can you tell us what happened, m'sieu? Is there danger?'

'Not immediate danger,' Dawlish said. He swung round to face Mademoiselle Blanc. 'Mam'selle!' he called. 'Where is the box?'

'In the taxi,' the woman called back. Her face looked strangely pale in the street lights, her eyes had a luminous glow.

'A moment,' Dawlish said, and looked back at the plain-clothes man. 'This container must be handled with great care. It should be taken to Orly or Le Bourget. I will take it from there to London.' There was so much to explain and so little time. If this man asked questions ...

'M. Ruhamel will be here very soon,' the man said.

No one asked what was in the container—but everyone was glancing towards the taxi, as if they had been warned.

'The explosion ...?' the plain clothes man began.

'A time-bomb. I put it in a bath.'

'You ...!'

'In the bath,' repeated Dawlish patiently. 'Now, will you please ...?'

There was a sudden outburst of talk by the old taxi, where four policemen stood on guard. Mademoiselle Blanc was speaking sharply and Dawlish caught the words: 'He must rest. He is exhausted.'

The plain-clothes man turned back to Dawlish. 'There is a bistro close by. If you will wait there, M. Dawlish, M. Ruhamel will join you.'

'It's urgent that I see him as soon as possible,' said Dawlish. By jove, he thought, the girl was right. He *was* tired. His whole body seemed to ache but until that moment he had not realised it. Suddenly everything swam in front of him.

The plain-clothes man gripped his arm as Mademoiselle Blanc pushed her way forward.

'I'm all right,' Dawlish muttered. 'The container ...'

'It will be protected,' the plain-clothes man assured him. 'And when M. Ruhamel arrives I will tell him of your instructions. Already we have been told to be very careful not to jolt it.'

'*Jolt* it!' exclaimed Dawlish, everything springing sharply back into focus. '*Jolt* it! My God, don't *touch* it! Leave it in the taxi.'

'We shall, m'sieu.'

'Please,' Mademoiselle Blanc said, pleadingly.

She took Dawlish's free arm, and together she and the plain-clothes man steered him across the street towards a red cigar sign, the word *Tabacs* glowing dully. Two gendarmes and the old taxi driver followed them; another gendarme already waited by the door.

The bistro was small, but warm and bright and clean. An array of multi-coloured bottles gleamed behind the polished counter, watched over by a young waiter with black, golliwog hair. Further along, a waitress leaned over an espresso coffee machine; cups were spread out on the bar, a jug of cream stood close by. One of the gendarmes cleared two chairs away from a table, and Dawlish sat down with plenty of room to stretch his legs.

Was the ingot in that box? he wondered.

The only way to find out was to examine the box itself, and that could only be done under conditions of extreme safety—at the Research Establishment, for instance. It would be as quick to go there as anywhere else, and an aircraft could land in those spacious grounds without difficulty. The more Dawlish thought, the more certain he became that this was the right thing to do. But would Ruhamel argue? he asked himself.

'You did not tell me I would be out so long, Marie,' grumbled the old taxi driver.

'I didn't know, Jules,' said Mademoiselle Blanc apologetically. She turned to a gendarme. 'Can the old one be taken home?'

'I don't want taking, I have my taxi.'

'That must stay here, Jules.' The woman looked at the plain-clothes man who seemed to be in charge, while the waitress placed a steaming cup of coffee topped with cream in front of Dawlish.

'You wish for something to eat, m'sieu?'

'Is there—fresh bread?'

'Yes, sir.'

'Take the old one home,' the plain-clothes man was saying.

'With plenty of butter,' said Dawlish.

It was all so mixed up he thought, this combination of the homely, the absurd, and the deadly. Outside was a container the contents of which could reduce everyone here to ashes. At the door was the old man, grumbling as he was led out. The golliwog-haired young man was handing small glasses to two policemen, the woman was now standing by Dawlish's side.

'Please sit down,' Dawlish said gently.

'I am not in the way?' asked Marie Blanc.

'No,' said Dawlish. 'Not now or any time. I owe you too much. That was very brave of you,' he added, as she sat beside him.

'It was nothing.'

'My instructions,' said the plain-clothes man, ruefully, 'were to ask no questions.' He stood over the table, fine brown eyes asking the questions for him.

Dawlish looked up. 'Mademoiselle Blanc knew there was great danger, but came to help me. If it had not been for her, the container would have been blown open.'

'*Mon Dieu!*' gasped the plain-clothes man, and crossed himself.

'Is it so dangerous?' The waitress was putting coffee in front of Marie Blanc as she spoke.

'Yes,' Dawlish told her flatly.

'I did not know, so it was not so brave,' she murmured.

'To face the unknown is always brave,' said Dawlish. The sense of urgency had receded to the back of his mind, and he was beginning to enjoy the warmth and comfort of the bistro. The coffee was hot, the bread fresh, the pale butter delicious. Gradually the tension and the tiredness eased out of him.

Suddenly there was a commotion at the door, and Ruhamel arrived, tired-eyed, clean-shaven, somehow remote. With a curious kind of arrogance he looked about the room and the gendarmes seemed to melt away. He crossed to Dawlish, and the plain-clothes man bowed with ostentatious deference. Marie Blanc began to get up.

Dawlish put a hand on her shoulder and pressed her back into her chair.

'Please make sure that Mademoiselle Blanc is given every assistance and courtesy,' he said.

'That will be assured,' Ruhamel promised.

'Thank you. And now ...'

Ruhamel listened to what Dawlish asked, and raised no objections at all.

*   *   *

Behind the small aircraft in which Dawlish flew, the sun was rising above the horizon, out of dark clouds. Ahead, the sky was startlingly bright and a pale moon showed; a star seemed to watch over them. Down below, the Channel appeared strangely silvered. Dawlish, in the small cabin, sat back with the container beside him.

Very soon they crossed the coastline of England. People were already astir in farm and field; at the windows of cottages and farmhouses, lights showed pale; cars that looked like toys moved along roads narrow as pencilled lines on green and brown patchwork. A little later the huge sprawling mass of Birmingham could be seen, smoke drifting sluggishly out of enormous stacks and from a myriad tiny chimneys. But the aircraft did not cross the Midlands metropolis—it headed steadily towards Nuneaton and the huge coal tips and the dead machinery of the mines.

Soon the white buildings of the Research Establishment loomed up. Near it, in a huge field, fire-engines waited, two white ambulances standing by.

The aircraft circled, preparing to land.

The first man Dawlish recognised, as they taxied safely to a standstill, was Jonah Cotton; and on the instant he was struck by the likeness of the man to Marie Blanc's son, Pierre.

*   *   *

Dawlish, two senior officials, and a French agent who had travelled in another aircraft, stood with Cotton in the laboratory where he had first discovered the deadly effects of the ingot's ray. He was dressed in a white smock, and wore rubber gloves—or gloves which looked like rubber. There was an alert, intense expression in his eyes; he was the same man who had been so sorry for himself in Dawlish's apartment yet there was something very different about him.

Here, he was a man of much greater stature.

Every movement he made with the manipulators was slow and studied and sure.

Everything happened as it had when he had first shown Mortimer the experiment—except that now he opened the container with manipulators inside a screened cage. Dawlish, who had never seen the ingot, held his breath.

'Are you sure it is safe?' muttered one of the officials.

'Of course it's safe,' said Cotton, impatiently. 'Keep quiet.'

The man drew in a sharp breath.

Slowly, very slowly, the lid of the container, secured by a safety catch which Cotton released with methodical care, began to open. At last the ingot became visible.

To the watchers, peering tensely through the thick protective windows of the screened cage, it looked unbelievably small; like a tiny piece of coke which could be balanced in an egg cup.

'Is *that* the ingot?' asked the man who had last spoken.

'It looks like part of it,' said Cotton.

The significance of the word 'part' impinged on Dawlish's mind but only in a remote way—the tension he felt at seeing the contents of the container for the first time overcame all other feeling. In his mind's eye there was a picture of a heap of ash which had been Cristal. How long ago that seemed! Cristal, and the ashes of the old woman and her dogs.

Cotton frowned. 'We'll soon know for certain.'

Inside the box, which was slowly raised from the level of the bench, an opening appeared; and almost at once the pink tip of a mouse's nose; its sleek head and pink eyes showed next, and it climbed nimbly over into the main container.

The gap closed behind it.

There was a moment of utter stillness, then, suddenly, the little creature began to crumple up. In a few moments there was only ash.

'*Mon Dieu!*' muttered one of the gendarmes.

Cotton looked at Dawlish.

'You certainly found part of it,' he said flatly, 'but only part. And the other part's just as dangerous. You know what this means, don't you?' he added. 'Someone who knows how to handle these things, and who has the equipment to do so, has broken the ingot in two.'

He stopped.

'So the other half's still in Paris,' Ruhamel said tautly.

'All I know is that the other half isn't here,' said Jonah Cotton.

16

ONE PART MISSING

Dawlish sat in a private room of the Leofric Hotel in Coventry, looking out on to the modern shops built around the ancient statue of Lady Godiva. Huge red buses lumbered round the square but there was little sound. Immediately opposite were two tall church spires, one the spire of a church which had survived the concentrated bombing of the war, the other the spire of the old cathedral, ruins beneath it on one side, the new cathedral on the other.

New and old.

A phoenix risen out of the ashes.

A city which had survived the shadow of war, symbol of a world which had lived through the shadow of death.

Why was the world for ever damned to live in danger of war and total annihilation? When was man going to understand the folly of short-term gains, the deadly potency of greed and cruelty and love of power, which held so surely the seeds of man's destruction?

And when was he, Patrick Dawlish, going to realise that a soliloquy on human pigheadedness wouldn't get him anywhere?

Half-angry with himself, half-amused, he turned away from contemplation of the two spires, and as he did so the telephone bell rang. He stretched out for the instrument.

'Dawlish.'

'Mr. Mellor is on his way up, sir.'

'Thanks,' Dawlish replaced the receiver and stepped to a door which communicated with the next room, tapped, and opened it. Ruhamel was lying on a bed, arms raised, head on his hands; his shoes were off and his tie was loose. So the man *was* human, thought Dawlish.

'The Minister of Defence will be here in a couple of

minutes,' he said. 'Did you sleep?'

'I am rested,' Ruhamel answered. Without shifting his position, he went on; 'M. Dawlish, I did you a grave injustice in Paris. I believed that you took too much upon yourself. Cristal had always told me you were a remarkable man in all ways—particularly in courage. I now agree with him absolutely.'

'You're very generous,' said Dawlish uncomfortably.

Ruhamel, studying him, gave a slow appreciative smile. He was still smiling when there was a knock at the door of Dawlish's room. Dawlish went to open it, and found Mellor and Professor Gordon Sanderson outside, two Special Branch men standing near by, and a deferential manager hovering respectfully behind them.

'Good morning, Dawlish.' Mellor's expression was stern, his voice clipped. So he was going to be formal, thought Dawlish.

'Come in, sir,' he said. 'Professor.' He smiled, ironically, at the man he had drugged the previous day.

They went inside and the Special Branch men took up their positions outside the door; Mellor's security men were never far away from him.

Dawlish turned to Sanderson. 'I hope you didn't suffer too much ill-effect from your sleep.'

'I am not interested in what happened yesterday—only in what we can do now,' said Sanderson stolidly.

'Good,' smiled Dawlish. 'May I introduce M. Ruhamel, Chief of Security in Paris?' he added, as the communicating door opened, and Ruhamel appeared.

There were handshakes and an exchange of courtesies. Then Mellor sat down, motioning the others to do the same.

'Like Professor Sanderson I have only one concern,' he began, 'and that is to find the other part of the ingot. I have studied your report, Mr. Dawlish. Do you think Mortimer knows where this other part is?'

'He could know,' said Dawlish slowly, 'but I've no idea whether he does.'

'Our people took him from the house in Rue Cabot,' Ruhamel put in. 'I would have been told had he made any useful statement.'

'Why don't we have him *here*?' demanded Sanderson. '*I* could deal with him.'

'We may have to try methods you wouldn't care about,' Dawlish said drily. 'How well do you know Eric Mortimer?'

'Very well.'

'And yet you believed him to be wholly reliable?'

Sanderson leapt to his feet; even standing while the others sat he did not seem tall, but there was a bull-like quality about his massive shoulders and thick neck.

'I resent that question,' he grated. 'It impugns my own integrity.'

'Professor ...' began Mellor, about to soothe the scientist.

'For the second time Dawlish has insulted me. He implies that I would employ a man *knowing* him to be unreliable.' Sanderson glowered angrily at Dawlish.

Ruhamel leaned back resignedly, his fingers beating a bored tattoo on the arms of his chair, while Mellor appeared to be struggling to contain his impatience.

'Mortimer has been selling the results of his own researches and of experiments at your establishment,' said Dawlish sharply. 'If you didn't suspect, you should have done. When national security is at stake, we can't afford senior executives who keep their eyes closed.'

A very faint smile curved Ruhamel's lips.

Mellor relaxed a little.

Sanderson stepped forward, his hand raised, as if he would strike Dawlish. His teeth were clenched, his jaws working.

'Did you know his habit of weekending in Paris?' demanded Dawlish.

'I did.'

'Did you check what he was doing?'

'I knew what he was doing.'

'You *knew* what he was doing?' asked Dawlish softly. 'You *knew* he met agents in Paris and sold them secrets which ...?'

'Minister!' cried Sanderson. 'This man is twisting everything I say!'

'Then why not straighten it out?' suggested Mellor,

mildly. 'I *did* understand you to say that you knew what Mortimer was doing.'

'I knew he was going to a brothel. I thought——' Sanderson gulped—' I thought he was simply relaxing after the strain of his work. That is something you laymen never understand, the strain under which nuclear physicists and other research scientists labour. Unless they can relax —relax completely at times—they would collapse under the stress of knowing that their discoveries could affect the whole future of the world. Could *destroy* the world.'

Sanderson began to walk up and down the room, his hands clenched, his heels thumping on the carpeted floor.

'A man in my position has to allow for this,' he went on. These men *must* relax. Some can, and do, with their families. Some, with sport and hobbies. Some with women. I considered Mortimer's Paris visits to be safety valves. I trusted him absolutely. That is why this—this revelation comes as such a shock.' He paused, wiping his forehead with the back of his hand, then sat down, as if his legs would no longer bear his weight. 'I can hardly believe it,' he said unsteadily. 'Had it been Cotton, I would have understood more easily. No wife, no family, no relaxation of any kind—the man's often worried me. Now if *he* had sold secrets ... But Mortimer—Mortimer a traitor!'

Dawlish leaned forward. 'I'm sorry, Professor, but I'm afraid it's an inescapable fact. Mortimer *is* a traitor. Now —it is likely, is it not, that *he* divided the ingot. You have examined the container?'

Sanderson nodded. 'Closely.'

'Is it one used here?—a ZIK?'

'It is.'

'So when Mortimer took the ingot, he may have taken two containers—may have even split the ingot before he left?' Again Sanderson nodded.

'But would it not take too long for him to do this here and remain undiscovered?' asked Ruhamel, spreading his hands apologetically.

'The ingot could be divided in fifteen minutes,' Sanderson stated flatly.

'So this could have been done while you were interviewing Cotton,' Dawlish reasoned.

'Easily.'

Ruhamel spoke again. 'Have Mortimer's movements immediately before he left this country been traced?'

'Partly,' answered Dawlish. 'My chief assistant carried out the investigation himself. Mortimer drove away from the Research Establishment at three-twenty-five p.m. He parked his car opposite the Nuneaton Public Library, where he was seen by a Nuneaton C.I.D. inspector who was passing, and was later seen by a police constable being driven away in a blue Zodiac. He left England on a Paris flight from Heathrow Airport, and the Zodiac was subsequently traced to London. We're still looking for the driver.'

'Thank you,' said Ruhamel.

'Mr. Dawlish,' said Mellor impatiently, 'how do these matters affect the recovery of the missing part of the ingot?' He turned to Sanderson. 'Presumably this is as deadly as the whole ingot?' he asked.

'It would probably have a smaller range of destruction,' Sanderson told him. 'Otherwise, it's just as dangerous.'

Dawlish looked thoughtful. 'There seems little doubt that whoever left part of the ingot in Paris intended its shadow to kill indiscriminately and so shock the world into realisation of the ingot's deadly powers—and the powers of whoever possessed the remaining part,' he finished grimly.

'Which means we must find this remaining part.' Mellor looked tense.

'We've something else to do as well, Minister,' said Dawlish slowly.

'What's that?'

'Well, sir, are we quite sure we can rely on Cotton? The Professor tells us that he has instinctive doubts. I have rational doubts. He could well be in collusion with Mortimer. Before we do anything else, we have to make sure that he isn't.'

'How can we possibly make sure that Cotton isn't working with Mortimer?' asked Sanderson.

'Have you *any* reason to think they may be working together?' asked Dawlish.

'No,' answered Sanderson. 'As a matter of fact, it always seemed as if they had a natural antipathy towards each other.'

Dawlish turned to Mellor. 'All our men, all European forces, all Intelligence Corps men from all nations, are working to trace the men Bruckner and Svensen. Everything which can be done to find them is being done. So my job is to concentrate on Mortimer and anyone who works or might work with him. Is that reasonable?'

Mellor nodded.

'M. Ruhamel arranged for Mortimer to be brought to England—he is here in Coventry now,' Dawlish went on. He turned back to Sanderson. 'Professor, I understand you have a laboratory with a one-way window through which the occupants can be observed from your office without their knowledge?'

'I arranged for the window myself,' said Sanderson, stiffly. 'A security measure.'

'I want you to give Cotton a job in that laboratory,' Dawlish told him. 'I would like him to carry out the experiment which led to his discovery of the deadly powers of the ingot. Can he repeat this?'

'According to what he has told me, yes,' said Sanderson. 'But what purpose ...?'

'We'll send Mortimer to join him, and see what happens,' interrupted Dawlish. 'We're twenty-five minutes' drive from the Research Establishment—we can see the outcome of this in less than an hour. Will you come with us, Minister?'

'Yes, indeed,' said Mellor. 'But will Mortimer co-operate?'

'He will be given an injection of ambutel which will create a temporary condition of amnesia,' said Dawlish. 'Unless Mortimer receives a very severe shock, which will bring him out of the amnesia, the events of the last twenty-four hours will be forgotten. He will behave exactly as he would have behaved prior to the theft of the ingot.'

'Ah-ha,' murmured Mellor. 'I'm beginning to understand. Less than an hour, you say ...'

It was, in fact an hour and a half later when Mellor,

Ruhamel, Sanderson, and Dawlish stood at the one-way window, watching Cotton in his mask and protective clothing, working at an oven which generated heat of over 6,000 degrees Fahrenheit. The cool deliberation which was characteristic of the man when working on an experiment had never been more in evidence, and watching the experiment was, in itself, hypnotically absorbing.

As Cotton closed the oven and stood back, the door of the laboratory opened, and Mortimer appeared.

17

CONFRONTATION

Jonah Cotton was fully aware of being watched.

Although it was supposed to be a secret, everyone in the Research Establishment knew about the one-way window; it was one of Sanderson's little tricks which everyone humoured. But Cotton had no idea why he had been asked to conduct this experiment, unless it was to make sure that the metals, gases, and chemicals used were exactly as he had described them. At the back of his mind there was a fear that Sanderson was finding a way to discredit him; since he, Cotton, had seen what Dawlish had done to him, Sanderson would be bitterly resentful.

The man in Cotton was filled with resentment, too. Against Sanderson; against Mortimer; against the world. He felt that he was the victim of an enormous conspiracy and that unless he was very careful, *he* would suffer.

Not Mortimer ...

God! How he *hated* Mortimer.

Gradually, these emotions faded as interest in the experiment quickened. It did not matter how often he carried out this—or any other—experiment, sooner or later his interest in it drew all bitterness out of him. In his laboratory, he was happy—end even with the fear of

113

losing his precious appointment, of being denied the laboratory and all the facilities he needed, what he was doing gradually drove everything else out of his mind.

He had done everything he should; the treated metal now needed heating for twenty minutes at a temperature of 6,200 degrees Fahrenheit. Until then he could take off his mask, and relax, though first he must place a protective screen round the oven, and get the claw manipulators ready to move the red-hot ingot.

He turned to press the switch which would set the protective cover in position, and saw a man at the door. Until that moment he had been so absorbed that he had heard and noticed nothing.

Was this Sanderson? he wondered.

No, it wasn't Sanderson, it was more like Mortimer.

It *was* Mortimer!

Closing the door behind him by presssing a button— now the laboratory was hermetically sealed, and there was not the slightest risk of anything from inside escaping and contaminating anything outside—Mortimer removed his mask and stepped forward, a smile on his face, his expression so normal it was almost impossible for Cotton to believe he was really there.

'How many more times will you have to do that experiment before you're satisfied?' he asked.

*   *   *

Every word, every sound, was audible to the men watching the one-way mirror. There was nothing they could miss.

*   *   *

Cotton did not speak, just stared at Mortimer, his expression one of utter idiocy. He knew what he looked like, knew that in some moods Mortimer would taunt him with it—Mortimer's attitude towards him had always been slightly derisory, slightly condescending, and because of this Cotton was usually on his guard. Now he stood and stared open-mouthed.

Mortimer, quite unabashed, moved closer towards him.

'I asked a simple question,' he said. 'How about a simple answer? Or has you life and death discovery made you even more stupid?'

The devil! thought Cotton, the treacherous devil!

'I always warned you not to work so hard,' Mortimer went on. 'You ought to have a few weekends off. You might even find a girl-friend—if you pay well enough,' he added waspishly. He drew level with Cotton in front of the oven, and then said as if with sudden understanding: 'Oh, now I see! Sanderson made you carry out an experiment under surveillance. He doesn't trust you. I wondered why he sent me in.'

At last Cotton spoke. 'How low can you sink?' he asked hoarsely.

'What's that? Take your mask off, man, take your mask off. You're grunting like a pig.'

Still speaking from behind his mask, Cotton said: 'How much did they pay you?'

Mortimer started.

'*What* did you say?'

'You heard me. How much did they pay you for stealing the ingot?'

Mortimer stood absolutely still: obviously appalled. In all the years they had worked together, Cotton had never known him to look like this—as if the ground had been swept from under his feet. Cotton felt a surge of triumph.

'Go on, tell me how much you got for selling your country's secrets. Tell me.' He raised a hand, and Mortimer backed away. '*Tell me how much you got and who paid you!*' shouted Cotton. 'If you don't ...!'

He broke off.

Suddenly, all the pent-up frustrations of years, combining with his disgust at Mortimer's treachery, swelled about him. Instead of moving nearer to Mortimer, he put a hand towards the switch which controlled the oven door. Outside, the door was cool, inside there was the raging furnace which was fusing those metals and gases into the horror that was the ingot.

'*Tell me who paid you or I'll open the oven!*' he cried.

*   *   *

'My God, he'll do it!' Mellor exclaimed. 'Stop him!'

'He's mad!' gasped Sanderson, swinging round. He snatched at a microphone which, when switched on, would carry his voice into the laboratory, but as he touched it Dawlish's fingers closed over his wrist and pulled his hand away. 'Let me go! He'll kill him!' cried Sanderson.

'Wait,' muttered Dawlish.

Ruhamel turned his gaze momentarily from the scene of high drama inside the laboratory to look at Dawlish's set face. He did not speak.

'We know now that Cotton's innocent,' said Mellor, thin-voiced. 'Mortimer might tell us more.'

'Cotton might do a better job of making him talk than we can,' Dawlish said flatly. 'Wait.'

'It's inhuman!' cried Sanderson.

'So is Mortimer,' said Dawlish.

*   *   *

Oblivious of what was going on outside, Jonah Cotton stood with his hand over the switch, watching Mortimer cringing away from him. Mortimer's face was twisted with fear, but Cotton did not realise that this fear was due as much to Mortimer's returning recollection as to Cotton's threat.

'Who did you sell out to, Mortimer?' he asked scornfully.

This time Mortimer did not hesitate to answer.

'Two—two men in Paris.'

'What men?'

'You—you wouldn't know them. One was—was named Bruckner, the other Svensen. Come—come away from that door.' Mortimer's voice shook, making his words almost inaudible. 'Please—please come away.'

'How much did you pay you?'

'Five—five thousand pounds.'

'For *my* secret, you . . .'

'They'd pay more,' Mortimer gasped. 'They'd pay you as much. I don't want to cheat you, I'll make them . . .'

'What makes you think I'd touch their money?' demanded Cotton. 'You may be handsome outside but you're rotten within. You're rotten, Mortimer, through and through. I always knew it or you couldn't have talked to me the way you have. And where did you meet these fine gentlemen?'

'I—I met them in a house in Paris. They—there are some girls there, Jonah, pretty girls, you'd like ...'

'You make me sick,' said Cotton slowly. 'Where are these men?'

'I—I don't know. They—they always send messages to me in Paris, No. 48, Rue Cabot. I don't go to them, they always come to me. That's all I know, Jonah, I swear it.'

'Then you aren't much use to anyone alive,' Cotton said, and his hand moved closer to the switch of the oven door.

'Don't open it!' screamed Mortimer. 'Don't—don't kill me, don't ...' He put his hands to his headpiece and tried to pull it over his face, but his whole body was so unsteady that he could not get it up.

Cotton moved away from the oven.

'Dawlish can deal with you better than I can,' he said quietly. '*He'll* fix you, Mortimer, I'll leave it to him. And thank God I'll never have to work with you again.'

*　　*　　*

Slowly, Dawlish's fingers slackened about Sanderson's wrist, but Sanderson made no attempt to speak over the microphone. Ruhamel smiled thinly, approvingly, at Dawlish. Mellor pursed his lips and wiped the sweat off his forehead.

'Apparently Mortimer can't help us any further.'

'Obviously he couldn't have known about the antique shop until today,' Dawlish said. 'We'll have to take it from there.' Bleakness sounded in his voice and showed in his eyes. 'We're not out of the wood yet by a long way. But there must be a line of inquiry from that shop.'

'Directly there is word, we will be told,' said Ruhamel.

'Who might know something?' asked Mellor.

'Mademoiselle Blanc perhaps,' Dawlish suggested. 'Or Mrs. Smithers—but I doubt, even if they *do* know anything, if either of them is aware of it.' He turned to Sanderson. 'Do you realise what a remarkable man Cotton is?'

'Yes,' muttered Sanderson, 'yes, indeed. I didn't realise it before, but I do now. He's—he's a very fine man. I'll see that he's rewarded, Dawlish. I'll recommend him for early promotion.'

'You could also try treating him as a human being,' Dawlish said coldly. 'But I'll need him for a few days on the investigation.' He looked hard into Sanderson's eyes. 'Is there anyone else in the Research Establishment who could possibly have been aware of Cotton's discovery and learnt how to handle the ingot?'

'I would have said it was impossible,' Sanderson answered. 'But if Mortimer didn't divide the ingot, well, someone else *must* have learnt how to handle it.'

*　　　*　　　*

'No one, absolutely no one,' said Cotton, when Dawlish asked him the same question.

'Nonsense,' said Dawlish emphatically.

They were together in a compartment of a train speeding from Nuneaton to London. Between them was a table, fitted into slots by the window; they had eaten a good lunch, and now empty coffee cups rattled in their saucers. Mellor had returned several hours earlier and Ruhamel had flown back to Paris, where he would intensify the search for Bruckner and Svensen. Every police force in the world had a red alert, so did every security force, and every Government knew of the danger.

Cotton's lips tightened as Dawlish said 'nonsense' with such emphasis, and his eyes narrowed. But he did not answer at once. He now knew that his confrontation with Mortimer had been deliberately arranged, and he also knew why. He had seen the chastened Sanderson for a few minutes, and had spoken to both the Minister for War and Ruhamel.

'You lost a key,' continued Dawlish.

'Mortimer took it,' said Cotton flatly.

'But it could also have been taken by someone else,' reasoned Dawlish. 'It could have been taken from Mortimer. To say it's impossible that anyone else could have been aware of what you discovered *is* nonsense.'

'I am a research physicist,' Cotton reminded him. 'Not a detective.'

'You have to find out all the facts and draw conclusions from them,' Dawlish said. 'The fact is that if there was a leakage, there could have been others.'

Cotton frowned. 'I don't think you're looking for your facts in the right place,' he said slowly.

'Where would you look?'

'In Paris.' Cotton had been told about the house in the Rue Cabot and of what had happened there. 'Surely the most important thing to do is to get hold of Bruckner and Svensen.'

'We're going to Paris,' Dawlish said. 'But I need to check with my London people first.'

Cotton leaned back in his seat, looking steadily at his companion.

'Why are you taking *me*, Mr. Dawlish?' he asked. 'Do you still have doubts?'

'Until I know the whole truth I have doubts of everyone,' Dawlish said. 'And I'm taking you because you're the one man in the world who can positively identify this particular ingot.'

Cotton did not shift his gaze. 'I don't believe you.'

'Why not?'

'There won't be any doubt about whether it's the original ingot—if it's in a protective container with the right code number. You don't need *me* to identify it. Why *do* you want me? There must be a powerful reason —unless there is, I am simply a liability. You don't trust me, do you? You want to make sure I can't contact anyone else without you knowing it.'

'I could use a dozen policemen for that,' Dawlish said. 'There isn't a thing you or I do which will be unobserved.' He smiled broadly. 'But you're quite right— there *is* another reason.'

'What is it?'

'You believe you're the only man in the world who

can make the ingot.'

'Yes.'

'Whoever paid Mortimer to steal the first may have use for more,' Dawlish pointed out. 'As I told you once before, you could be very valuable to them. You have discovered something at once deadly and unique. If I were Bruckner or Svensen I would plan to kidnap you—and if an attempt is made I want to be at hand,' he finished.

Cotton sat very still.

18

THE DANGER TO MARIE BLANC

Dawlish stood in his office at Scotland Yard. Childs and two assistants were with him, and Cotton was sitting in a corner, watching and listening with fascination. Calmly, quietly, Dawlish gave instructions, touching on every aspect of the situation, seeing every danger.

' ... If it was taken out of Paris by road it could now be as far away as Bonn, Zürich, Vienna, Milan, Barcelona, Madrid, Copenhagen, or places *en route* and of a similar distance ... If it was taken out by train, then every terminus in Europe except Moscow, Leningrad, Athens, or possibly Warsaw is within range ... If taken by air, it could be as far away as Buenos Aires, Johannesburg, Karachi, or New Delhi. Has every police force in the world been told ...?

'One of us has spoken to the chief of every force,' answered Childs.

'They've been given a full description of the container, weight, size, the lot?'

'Yes, sir.'

'Any reports come in, yet?'

'Twenty-seven—each a false alarm.'

'Are these reports from Paris and the nearer cities—Brussels, Amsterdam ...?'

'Every city is on the alert,' said Childs. He looked very tired, as if dealing with this emergency had sapped all his energy.

'The names Bruckner and Svensen ...'

'Every man and woman so named has been or is being checked throughout Europe and the United States.'

'Make it a general request to all police forces in the Conference,' Dawlish ordered.

'I'll do that,' promised Childs.

'Anyone of whom there is the slightest suspicion should be held and flown to Paris,' Dawlish went on. 'I'll be there, and you can get me through Ruhamel.'

'Yes, sir.' Childs paused. 'Do you know who will replace Cristal?' he asked.

Dawlish shook his head.

'I can hardly believe ...' began Childs, only to break off. 'Your chopper's ready, sir.'

'Thanks,' said Dawlish.

He led Cotton out of the room, and towards the car that was waiting to take them to the heliport on the river near Battersea Bridge. But it was not until they were flying over the huge stacks of the power station and the voluminous white smoke pouring out of each stack, that he spoke.

'Childs and Cristal of Paris were very old friends,' he said, turning towards Cotton.

'Childs looked ill,' Cotton remarked.

Dawlish frowned. 'I'm afraid he did—this affair has shaken him badly.' He closed his eyes as the helicopter roared over the south-eastern suburbs, seeing once again the heap of ash that had been Cristal ... and the heaps which had been an old woman and her two pet dogs.

They landed at a small airport in Kent, and took off again in a six-seater prop-jet for Paris. After the rambling fields of England the French countryside looked almost geometrical in design, and the tall trees lining the pale grey roads appeared so tiny that Dawlish could hardly believe they were real.

Soon, Paris loomed up, the Church of the Sacré Cœur showing strangely white in the bright sunlight, the Eiffel Tower looking like a child's toy.

They landed at Le Bourget, and Dawlish could almost see Cristal as he had approached him here a dozen times. Two police cars drew up close by the aircraft, and a man he knew slightly, Inspector Santot, came hurrying towards them. Santot was a big and ruddy-faced Frenchman, with sparkling blue eyes. Seeing these things, Dawlish also saw the alarm in the man.

'What is it?' he demanded.

'The son of Mademoiselle Blanc is missing,' Santot answered. 'Mademoiselle Blanc is in great distress.'

'And you think he may have been kidnapped to prevent his mother from telling us anything she knows?' asked Dawlish, after a startled silence. 'Is that it?'

'But of course, m'sieu. And we must find a way to make her talk.'

*   *   *

The kidnapping had happened only half an hour or so earlier.

The police were watching the Rue Cabot from both ends, and from roof-tops and windows and doorways along the street itself. A helicopter hovered, its engine noisy and harsh, and photographs were taken almost continually. And although the antique shop had been gutted by fire, the same precautions were being carried out in the Rue des Saints Pères.

Anyone who approached No. 48, Rue Cabot was watched, and questioned after leaving.

Mademoiselle Blanc was questioned almost without stopping by different officers, but she always gave the same answers. The owner of 48, Rue Cabot was a man named Martel. Martel paid her a small wage to look after the house, and telephoned her with instructions to give all facilities to certain men. She was allowed to let off rooms whenever they were free.

The Paris and Rouen police were searching for Martel; so far there was no word of him.

Most of the time the boy, Pierre, had sat with his mother, terrified. Every now and again she had to re-assure and pacify the child, and eventually he was allowed to go into the street and along to the boulevard.

Pierre loved the roar and the sound and the bustle, the lights and the colours. He was known to everyone who lived near by, ignored by most, given sweets or chocolate by a few. And one or two old women who scraped sub-sistence out of the waste from the shops and the dustbins, would sometimes talk to him in a kind of pidgin French, which they all seemed to understand, including Pierre.

The police were not interested in such a boy.

Most of them were repelled by his appearance.

No one suspected he might be used.

Now, one of the old women came up to him, and after a while they walked together away from the Rue Cabot. No one took any notice of them. The woman was fat and shapeless, with swollen legs and ankles, and wearing ragged clothes and down-at-heel shoes. Together they shuffled through the narrow French streets, until the boy, out of his usual and familiar surroundings, began to grizzle. The old woman took him by the hand and, re-assured, he turned with her into a courtyard not unlike his own.

A man came from the concierge's office.

'This is the boy?'

'It is Pierre Blanc, yes.'

'From 48, Rue Cabot?'

'All my life I have known him,' the old woman said, indignantly. 'Would I lie to you?'

'For twenty francs you would lie to *le bon Dieu*,' the man retorted. He gave her twenty one-franc coins, drop-ping them into her outstretched palms. The boy's eyes glistened; he had never known so much money. The man turned to him.

'Would you like one?'

Pierre gave an excited squeal.

'Does he understand me?' the man asked the old woman.

'He knows what money is, don't you doubt.'

'Will he do what he is told?'

The old woman nodded. 'Yes—if he understands.'

'I want him to give some of these to his mother,' the man told her.

'So! He will understand *me*.' She held out her hands again and the boy's eyes darted towards the man, who took more coins from his pocket, and placed one in the old woman's hands.

'That is for him to spend,' he said. '*That* one—make him understand.'

The old woman talked to the boy in the curious argot he understood so well, and almost at once he nodded, eagerly. She gave him the coin and he held it on the palm of his hand and gloated over it, his eyes as bright as the new franc piece.

'And these two are for your mother,' said the concierge, holding out two more coins.

'*Pour ta mère*,' the old woman said. '*Maman*.' And she repeated '*Maman*' over and over again. The boy nodded, and she tucked the coins inside the pocket of his faded blue blouse. Pierre gave them a little pat, and then looked at his own coin, enraptured.

'For Pierre,' said the man, looking very pleased with himself, and gave the boy yet another.

Pierre stared as if he could not believe in such munificence, then cupped the coins in both hands and jingled them together.

'Like music,' the man said, and laughed. 'Here's another for *Maman*.'

The old woman tucked this one away with the others.

'That is all.' The man patted the boy's head, then turned to the old woman. 'He can spend some of his own on the way back,' he told her, 'but he *must* be in his own home in half an hour. Is that clear?' He paused, looking at her sharply before adding: 'No later.'

'Is it so important?' the old woman demanded.

'There is an important message for his mother in the coins, and the time is very important indeed.'

'He will be there in good time,' the old woman promised.

'Then start now,' the man urged her.

The old woman led the boy off. At a café round the

corner she allowed him to buy ice-cream. He stared at the change in even greater amazement and delight, then stopped jingling it and held it tightly in one hot hand while he held the ice-cream in the other, licking, eating, smearing lips and nose and chin.

He had never been so happy.

*   *   *

The man who had given the money away went back into the concierge's office, reappearing a few minutes later without the concierge's uniform he had been wearing. Now he was smartly though inconspicuously dressed in the dark, well-cut suit of the average French businessman. Walking briskly towards the boulevard, he stopped at a telephone kiosk, and made a call.

A man answered.

'Is that you, Philippe?'

'Yes,' said the dark-suited man. 'The boy has the coins. The house will blow up in forty-five minutes from now.'

'Wait there until the explosion,' ordered the man at the other end of the telephone. 'Then report again. You were not followed?'

'No.'

'The boy?'

'Who would take any notice of an imbecile?' demanded the man in the dark suit. 'And who would expect three shiny francs to have enough explosive to ... ?'

'*Imbecile!*' the other man cried. 'The operator could be listening.'

But no one listened.

*   *   *

Dawlish sat with Cotton and Santot in the police car as it sped towards the Porte d'Orléans. The Paris suburbs were hot in the sunlight, the street markets bright and gay with umbrellas and awnings, the traffic noisy and thick. Now and again a message came over the radio, but there was nothing of importance until they were only five minutes away from the Rue Cabot. Then a note of excitement sounded in a man's voice, and Dawlish leaned forward.

'The child, Pierre, is back,' explained Santot.

'At home?' demanded Dawlish.

' ... On the corner of the street ...' a man said over the air.

'How long has he been away?' asked Dawlish.

'An hour, perhaps a little more.'

'We want to find out where he went,' began Dawlish. Then they heard the man's voice over the transmitter: '... his face covered with ice-cream ...'

'So he went to spend his pocket money,' observed Santot.

Dawlish sat back, frowning, and Cotton looked at him as if puzzled by his expression. Soon, they turned into the Rue Cabot, and four gendarmes moved aside the wooden barricades. The pulled up outside No. 48, which was tall and narrow and drab, even in that poor district. Police filled the tiny courtyard; more police waited in the narrow hallway, and were stationed on the winding staircase.

There was a sound of scolding from a room on the first floor.

'Where have you been, Pierre?' It was Marie Blanc. 'And look at you—*look* at you!' She seemed to round on someone else who was with her, her voice shrill with indignation. 'Who let him stay out for so long? Who gave him money to buy ice-cream?'

'Ice-cream won't hurt him,' a man said soothingly.

'He will be sick, he is always sick after eating ice-cream!' the woman cried.

When Dawlish and Cotton and Santot entered the room she was kneeling beside the child, looking accusingly over his shoulder at two police officers. Dawlish had never seen a child in such a mess; ice-cream was smeared all over the once clean blouse, there were even little icicles of it dangling from his eyebrows. He stood looking at his mother, half-frightened, half-eager, then took something out of his blouse pocket.

'Maman,' he said huskily.

'Oh, what is it?' demanded his mother. She was haggard from the lack of sleep, and there were great shadows under her eyes, which looked bright as glass. She had clearly slept in her clothes, her face was shiny and her hair uncombed. She was distraught, yet obviously fighting to control herself in front of the child.

Slowly, proudly, Pierre placed two shiny francs on the palm of his hand and held them out to her.

'*Maman*,' he said, quite clearly. '*Pour Maman*.'

And he smiled.

Despite the ice-cream which smeared his face, despite the tiny eyes and the thick lips and the malformed body, there was dignity in him, born of the pleasure he derived from offering this gift.

19

RADIANCE

Over the world a dark shadow lay.

Over Paris and its people the shadow was closer and darker and more menacing, and there was no certainty that it would not fall upon the young and the innocent, the good as well as the bad.

Only a few people knew of the danger, and perhaps no one was more intensely aware of it than Dawlish and Cotton—and on the journey Dawlish had come to believe just how deeply Cotton felt his responsibility.

Dawlish believed the danger to be very close—to be here, perhaps in this very room. He did not then suspect where it lay, only that the danger might come with the opening of a door, as softly and as silently as a shadow could fall anywhere.

Yet he watched Pierre and saw the pride in the boy's face, the new, unsensed pride; the pleasure. Watching, he forgot the nearness of impending disaster and his own tension, for he saw also the woman's face. Weary from

127

being questioned all night, hungry, frightened, she had been sharp-tongued and impatient with her child, but now the frown and the furrows were smoothed away and the vexation died out of her eyes. In those few seconds, she seemed younger, much younger; a girl.

She smiled, too, and held out her hand for the gift; then, since Pierre's remained upturned, she took the francs.

'*Merci, mon chéri*,' she said.

For a moment, no one moved. Then, suddenly, the spell seemed to fall from Marie Blanc, and she was aware of the others, watching. Once again, the years weighed heavily upon her. Dawlish sensed that she was half-expecting ridicule because she had taken the francs and not boxed the child's ears and asked him where he had found them.

She glanced at Dawlish in a curious kind of aggressive defensiveness—then at Jonah Cotton, who was by Dawlish's side.

She was startled; and so was Dawlish, by the change in her.

He looked at Cotton.

He did not think—when afterwards he began to recollect that strange moment—that he would ever see such radiance again. For in Cotton's eyes, radiance glowed. He was staring at the mother and child, a couple whom most people would have passed with averted gaze; and he was radiant. It dawned on Dawlish, very slowly, that the man was looking at the kind of face he knew so well in the mirror; that there was nothing even faintly repellent to him, in Pierre.

No other word was said, but Pierre, seeing his mother's expression, turned his over-large head and looked at Cotton, shoulders beginning to hunch, body beginning to cringe. But he did not cringe. Something in Cotton's expression reassured him, and he turned and dug again into his blouse, bringing out the third coin and holding it towards his mother.

'*Pour Maman*,' he repeated gravely.

As gravely, his mother took it.

The child was satisfied, but not Marie—Dawlish saw

her bewilderment.

'Pierre—where ... ?'

'*Pour Maman,*' he repeated yet again.

'Yes,' she said hesitantly, but this time her smile was forced. 'Where did you get this money, Pierre?'

He did not answer; possibly he did not understand. 'Pierre ...'

'Don't worry him now, mademoiselle.' Dawlish kept his voice pitched low, and nothing in his facial expression or his tone was in key with the words which followed. 'Do you know where Pierre has been?'

She answered in English. 'No. He is not often away so long.'

'Has he been given money before?'

'Never a whole franc. A few centimes, sometimes.'

Dawlish frowned. 'We don't want to alarm him, but we ought to know where he's been and who gave him the money.' Even as he spoke, Dawlish felt dissatisfied; there was something he had missed, something that was eluding him. 'Do you think you can find out?' he asked.

'If he is not frightened.'

'There are too many people here,' put in Cotton, and Marie Blanc shot him a grateful glance. 'Can't we leave them alone, Dawlish?'

'Yes, for a while.' Dawlish led the way out of the room, and Santot followed, with the two policemen. Cotton closed the door, reluctantly. Dawlish was still dissatisfied and uneasy, but without knowing why.

Voices sounded below.

'Keep them quiet or they'll scare the wits out of the kid,' Cotton said.

'*Silence!*' Santot hissed over the balusters, and then led the way down the curved staircase. A man was speaking in a low-pitched voice but each word was clearly audible; so were those of another man, questioning him.

'... talked to the woman,' the first man was saying.

'What did she say?'

'She took the youth to a courtyard near Benedict's café.'

'Why?'

'She said a man wanted to send a gift to Mademoiselle

129

Blanc.'

'What man?'

'A stranger to her.'

'Where *is* this woman?' demanded Santot, on the bottom step.

'She is outside,' the man answered.

'What are they talking about?' asked Cotton irritably.

'A woman took Pierre to see a man who wanted to give his mother money,' translated Dawlish.

'Well?'

Dawlish spoke slowly, almost fearfully: 'Why this morning, of all mornings? Why give her money through the child?' No one answered him, the tone of his voice was so forbidding. 'Why use the *child*? ... Obviously because *he* might be allowed to leave the house ... and he was ... My God!'

'What is it?' Cotton demanded harshly.

'M. Dawlish ...' began Santot.

But Dawlish was now halfway up the stairs. Closely followed by Cotton, he raced towards the room they had just left and flung open the door. Inside Marie Blanc was wiping the dried ice-cream from the child's face.

'A strange man gave him those francs,' she told him. 'He didn't steal them.' She looked quite calm as she glanced up at Dawlish.

'Where are they now?' Dawlish demanded.

'In my pocket.' She tapped her side.

'Will you give them to me?' Dawlish asked. 'I will replace their value, if I have to take them away.'

'As you wish.' She finished with the boy and gave him a little shove. He made grumbling sounds but did not protest. She waited until his back was turned, then handed over the coins. Dawlish looked down at them, feeling the serrated edges. He was not used to French money these days, but the first coin seemed unusually thick; so did the second; so did the third.

'*What is it?*' hissed Santot, who had come into the room behind them.

'I want to be taken to a park or a piece of open ground,' said Dawlish. 'Is there one near?'

'There is an empty site where a new block of flats is

to be built,' a gendarme volunteered.

'Near?'

'Very near—only round the corner.'

'Take me there, quickly.'

'You think there might be *explosive* in the coins?' Santot demanded.

'It's possible.'

'M. Dawlish,' Santot said, 'I will take them, please. *Do not argue!*' he added sharply, and he took the coins from Dawlish's hands. Pushing Dawlish and Cotton aside, he bounded down the stairs. 'This empty site,' they heard him call, 'where is it? ... To the right, good ... Keep away from me, all of you ... Protect your faces ...' Above the sound of his voice came that of other men, giving orders; then footsteps on the cobbles.

'My God, what courage!' exclaimed Cotton. 'But do you really believe ... ?'

'Do you think I'd make a fuss if I didn't?' Anxiety made Dawlish's voice sharp. 'If they *did* try to blow this place up, or burn it down ...'

'Then the secret *is* here!' exclaimed Cotton.

'Yes,' muttered Dawlish. Why would anyone do this, he thought, except to keep Marie Blanc quiet? He reached the street in time to see Santot disappearing round a corner, one man with him, several others drawing back. He paused, Cotton close behind him.

More plain-clothes men turned into the street.

Then a car came round the corner and stopped; three men got out, two of them handcuffed together, followed by a shapeless old woman. For the first time since he had begun to suspect what might be in the coins, Dawlish forgot them, thinking: Who is the prisoner?

'This is the man,' one of the men was saying, 'who gave the money to ...'

His words were lost in a sudden roar, loud enough to drown every other sound. Cotton caught his breath. Dawlish looked for a moment as if he would strike the prisoner, but he spun round and began to run towards the scene of the explosion. Smoke was billowing from behind the roofs, pale grey in the sunlight.

Then Santot appeared at the corner, dishevelled and

dirty but walking very rapidly and obviously not hurt. He gave Dawlish a sharp glance.

'So you were right. But why should they wish to kill Marie Blanc?'

'Your men have caught the man who gave the boy the coins,' Dawlish said. 'Let's go and question him.'

The man, who had seemed so pleased with himself when he had dealt with Pierre, now crouched back against the wall fearfully. His name, he had already admitted, was Philippe Duval.

'He wanted to burn the house down,' he said. 'He wanted to kill everyone in it, that's all I know.'

'Who is *he*?' demanded Santot, harshly.

'My—my employer, m'sieu.'

'You allow your employer to command you to commit murder?'

'M'sieu, he would kill me,' Duval said simply. 'He has in his possession a box which, if opened, can spread death.'

'Who is *he*?' repeated Santot, with a sideways glance at Dawlish.

'I do not know,' the prisoner answered.

'But you have seen him, have you not?'

'No, m'sieu, never, I swear it. He talks to me only on the telephone, when he gives me his orders. This time he told me to destroy this house and the people in it.'

'Did he give you any other orders?' demanded Dawlish.

'He told me to make sure I killed Mademoiselle Blanc,' Duval replied. 'He told me that if she remained alive, then *I* would die. And I tell you, he has the power of life and death. I am not lying, m'sieu! It is true.'

'I believe you,' said Dawlish heavily. 'Did he tell you *why* Mademoiselle Blanc was to die?'

'No, m'sieu. But why should he wish that unless she was a grave danger to him?'

20

'GRAVE DANGER'

Dawlish stood by the window of the room in which he had first found Mortimer, looking through a gap in the houses to the site where the coins had exploded. Smoke still arose from rubble and old timbers which had been set on fire. Cotton was sitting tense and upright in a corner. The door was closed, but two gendarmes stood by it, ready to protect Dawlish should there be any further attack. On a table, close at hand, stood a two-way radio—tuned to ensure that he could be called, or could make a call, at any moment.

Everything that had happened passed through Dawlish's mind like pieces in a mental jigsaw puzzle which did not yet fit. But they *must* fit. He knew who had taken the ingot from the Research Establishment. He knew the two meeting places in Paris. He knew that men calling themselves Bruckner and Svensen did in fact exist. And he knew that someone had wanted to kill Marie Blanc, because 'she was a grave danger'.

She *must* be.

She had been questioned throughout the night by teams of expert interrogators and he had their reports here, spread out on the bed in the corner. Every report said the same thing: she kept this house for a man named Martel whom she had never seen. He paid her little, and she made what extra money she could, to support herself and the child, by letting any unoccupied rooms.

Time and time again she had been questioned: 'Who is the owner? Who is the man who telephones you?' And her reply had always been the same: 'I only know that he tells me his name is Martel.'

'Why do you look after such a house for so little pay?'

'Where else would I be able to keep my child with me?'

'Why do you not put the child in a home?'

'Where would I find the money—and what would Pierre do?'

Die, probably, of a broken heart. Or was that sheer sentiment? Dawlish wondered. He was aware of Cotton staring at the back of his head, and turned slowly. Cotton was putting one of the reports down. That cold, calculating, scientific mind might perceive something which he, Dawlish, had not seen, but nothing in Cotton's expression gave him any hope.

He must question Marie Blanc himself, but before he did so, he must think of a form of question which differed from those flung at her during the night, one which would not immediately cause resentment. What *was* the true explanation of her loyalty to Pierre, for instance. Mother-love? *Was* it possible to love such a child?

Cotton was staring at him almost as if he were reading his thoughts, and resenting them. The question was valid, all the same, and it set his mind in a different direction. Marie Blanc had affection for Pierre, she was patient and understanding and protective, but—was it love for the child? Or love for the man with whom she had conceived it?

'What diabolical idea have you got now?' demanded Cotton.

'What's that?' Dawlish asked absently.

'I can see from your eyes you're ready to knife someone.'

'What you should be doing is helping me sharpen the knife,' said Dawlish. 'I think . . .'

The radio bleeped, and a man said: 'There is a call for you from London, M. Dawlish.'

Was it from Childs? wondered Dawlish. He drew a little closer, and pressed a switch. 'This is Dawlish.'

'Childs here, sir. I now have the final reports on Mrs. Smithers, Major Hordle, and Wanda Hordle.'

'Yes?'

'There isn't the slightest indication that Mrs. Smithers is involved any more deeply than we knew before,' stated Childs. 'Or that Hordle is involved at all.'

There was no point in arguing, Dawlish thought; he must accept this as certain.

'Mortimer?' he asked.

'A little more, sir,' said Childs. 'A man, presumably Mortimer, sometimes received telephone calls from Paris while he was at Miss Hordle's apartment—we've checked that through the telephone exchange.'

'Any Paris calls to the Research Establishment? Or calls from any place near Paris?'

'None for Mortimer, sir.'

'Any at all?'

'Yes—from the Nuclear Establishments at Orly and near Versailles,' Childs told him. 'These are frequent, though, because there is a great deal of joint research.'

'Anything else at all helpful?' asked Dawlish.

'No, sir. Mortimer has broken down completely. If he knew the identity of Bruckner and Svensen I think he would have told us by now. I've spent an hour with him myself, and I don't think there is the slightest hope of getting anything more from him.'

'What about security at the Research Establishment?' Dawlish asked.

'Well, they slipped up badly on Mortimer, sir—he seems to have fooled security as completely as he fooled Sanderson.'

'As completely as he fooled Sanderson,' Dawlish repeated slowly. 'I wonder. I'm not at all happy ...'

A man broke across his words, voice raised with an excitement which was touched with fear.

'M. Dawlish—listen, please. There is a disaster near the Bastille—in the streets, m'sieu, people have died ...'

*   *   *

The man who first gave the alarm lived in a small apartment at the top of a new block of flats close to the Place de la Bastille. On that morning it was particularly crowded; a thousand people seemed to be going in a dozen directions at once. Then, suddenly some began to fall.

At first, the man—Jean Lesœur—thought that someone had fallen and made others stumble and fall, but no one attempted to get up. They lay still—then, before Jean Lesœur's horrified gaze, they began to disintegrate.

A man and two schoolboys were the first to fall; then two women; then a policeman on traffic duty. He gave a

shrill blast of his whistle, waved his white truncheon—
and fell, and crumpled up.

A car swerved across the road and crashed into others
parked by the kerb; the driver collapsed ...

A dozen drivers, a hundred men and women, collapsed ...

Jean Lesœur, telling the police by telephone from the
block of flats, described the scene as it was described to
Dawlish a few minutes later.

'It was as if a great shadow had passed over them, and
everyone it fell upon, just—just disintegrated ...'

As soon as the terror was over and the Place de la
Bastille was cordoned off, the police were able to assess
the situation. It was as if a huge segment had been cut out
of the air at ground level. It was possible to stand at the
very spot where a man or woman must have stood and
opened the container. No one above ground level
was touched, but the effect of the shadow stretched far
beyond the Place de la Bastille in an ever-widening arc.

It stopped at the banks of the river.

Everyone at the perimeter of the arc on the right bank,
died.

Everyone on the left bank lived; and life went on as if
there were no awareness of the disaster.

*　　　*　　　*

Almost as soon as the news arrived, coded cables and
telephone and radio-telephone calls reached Dawlish's
London office, the Paris offices of the Crime Haters, and
this little house of ill-repute so close to la Porte d'Orléans.
They came from Crime Haters in other countries,
from statesmen and politicians, from all who knew of the
horror and the danger, and they all asked the same thing
but in different words.

'*Do you know who is behind it, Dawlish?*'

*　　　*　　　*

Marie Blanc knew what had happened, and the
knowledge showed in the shadows of her eyes and her

136

tension, which somehow refined her features and smoothed her skin, making her look strangely like a two-dimensional portrait by an old Italian master. Cotton and Ruhamel were with Dawlish when he questioned her.

'Pierre's father?' she echoed quietly. 'He is dead, m'sieu. He died of the disease which made Pierre sick.'

'How long ago did he die?' asked Dawlish.

'A little more than ten years,' she answered.

'What work did he do?'

'Had he lived,' Marie answered proudly, 'he would have been a very great artist, m'sieu. He was too poor to pay for the food and medicines he needed. But why do you wish to know this?'

'I wanted to make sure you couldn't be lying for him or hiding him,' Dawlish said. 'Can you leave Pierre with neighbours for a day?'

Alarm sparked in her eyes.

'No, m'sieu. He would be terrified! Is it necessary for me to go to prison?'

Dawlish laughed at the unexpected fear.

'No, no,' he said reassuringly, 'I just want you to come to England with me to see a certain man. I'd like you to tell me whether he has ever stayed, or ever called, at this house.'

'Can he not come here?'

'If I send for him he may guess why,' Dawlish told her. 'At the moment he has no suspicion and will be waiting for me.'

Cotton took a step forward.

'I think Pierre would stay with me,' he said diffidently.

Startled, the woman turned towards him.

'It is possible, perhaps.' She sounded doubtful.

'Don't you want to come back with me?' Dawlish asked Cotton.

'Can it make any difference?' the physicist asked. 'I know who you mean, of course,' he added, without waiting for a reply. 'You have a remarkable mind, Dawlish. You eliminate every man in turn until you reach the one who cannot be eliminated. But why do you need Marie?'

'If I am right, he is more likely to confess if he is taken

137

by surprise,' said Dawlish. 'And I shall see that Mademoiselle Blanc *does* take him by surprise. Mademoiselle, is it possible for you to be ready to leave in half an hour? ... Thank you. M. Ruhamel, forgive me if I am discourteous, but I need to get to the airport as quickly as possible.'

He turned to the radio, flicked it on, and called Childs. 'Childs, I want to pay a surprise visit to the Midlands Research Establishment, but it *must* be a surprise visit. On no acount must anyone at the Establishment, including Sanderson, know of this ... What, he's just flown in from Paris? I thought he might have done ... No, never mind ... Yes, I'll take Mellor with me ... Right ... Yes, in about three hours ...'

*   *   *

Exactly three hours later, Dawlish, followed by Marie Blanc, Ruhamel, and Mellor, strode past the startled security guards and into Sanderson's private office. The office door had been locked, but this presented Dawlish with no problem. A few seconds' deft manipulation with a small steel instrument he had taken from his pocket, and it had swung open. Quickly, he led Marie Blanc towards the one-way window looking into Sanderson's security laboratory.

Dawlish's heart missed a beat. He was acting on a hunch—and it looked as though the hunch had paid off.

Sanderson was bending over the oven; and on the bench was a container identical to the one that was missing.

Dawlish drew Marie closer.

'Take your time,' he told her. 'Have a good look. Now —have you ever seen that man before?'

Marie Blanc looked carefully through the one-way window. Then she drew back.

'But yes, m'sieu, that man comes often to my house. But I have never spoken with him. He is always accompanied, and his visits are short.'

'Listen to his voice,' said Dawlish, and pressed a switch.

'Professor Sanderson,' he called.

Sanderson turned sharply.

'Who—who is that? where are you? You—you've no right . . . !'

'But that is the voice of the man who telephones me!' gasped Marie Blanc.

Dawlish gripped her arm. 'Are you certain?'

'But yes, that is M. Martel, there is no doubt about it.'

'Then we'll go in and see M. Martel,' said Dawlish. 'Stay behind me.' He led the way into the laboratory, his broad shoulders screening her completely.

Sanderson took a step towards him. His face was pale, his eyes were staring.

'Mr. Dawlish, I must protest. How did you get in? Why are you here?'

'Why do you think?' demanded Dawlish, and he stood aside.

Sanderson gasped, looking from Dawlish to Marie Blanc, then again to Dawlish. Suddenly he spun round.

'Keep away!' he cried. 'Keep away, or I'll open the container. I'll kill you both, I'll . . .'

He snatched at the container but missed it, and, as Dawlish sprang forward, it slid along the bench near the oven, dangerously close to the edge.

Dawlish hit the man beneath the chin with a blow which sent him halfway across the room. Then, very gingerly, he pushed the container back into a more secure position. Sanderson made no attempt to get up. Dawlish released the door control, and Ruhamel led in the police and laboratory workers.

*   *   *

When the container was examined, it proved to hold the missing section of the ingot stolen from Cotton's laboratory.

*   *   *

Ruhamel, Dawlish, and Marie Blanc were back in Paris late that night—a Paris stunned by the tragedy of the morning, but still gay and bright and very beautiful. Ruhamel had gone straight to his office—then, an hour or so later, he had joined the others at 48, Rue Cabot.

Cotton had put Pierre to bed and was now sitting next to Marie on a shabby, cotton-covered divan, while Dawlish leant back in an armchair, which, big though it was, was only just big enough to encompass his huge frame.

This was the first time he had been able to relax since the formalities were over and the arrests made. He leant back still further, stretching out his long legs in front of the fire which Cotton had miraculously fanned to life in the small grate.

'It had to be someone with facilities for splitting the ingot and handling it safely,' he said, almost musingly. 'Someone who knew Mortimer well, and who could give him the opportunity to steal the container. Someone responsible for security at the Research Establishment, yet who could appear to be fooled by one man, so that suspicion would fall on that man and not on him. It was this which first made me wonder about Sanderson. How was it that anyone so outstandingly efficient could allow Mortimer to get away with it? The answer was simple: because he wanted Mortimer to get away with it.

'Mortimer was the perfect dupe, working with men who were accomplices of Sanderson without suspecting Sanderson's complicity. It was Sanderson, of course, who arranged Wanda Hordle's murder, so pointing the accusing finger straight at Mortimer.

'There's a lot more to find out,' he added. 'Who exactly are Bruckner and Svensen, for instance, and who drove Mortimer away in that Zodiac? There's probably a great deal we'll never know—though much of it will come out at the trial. But the most important thing is that we've got the ingot—the whole ingot—*and* the two madmen who were trying to use it.'

Ruhamel leaned forward. 'Like so many things, Dawlish, once you have the key it's easy to see the answers. Finding the key is the great difficulty. I have to confess once again that I did not at first trust poor Cristal's judgment of you. But I do now.'

'He's got it all,' said Cotton unexpectedly. 'Looks,